T0005780

By John Wyndham

The Day of the Triffids
Foul Play Suspected
The Kraken Wakes
The Midwich Cuckoos
The Outward Urge
Plan for Chaos
Stowaway to Mars
Trouble with Lichen
Web

TROUBLE with LICHEN

JOHN WYNDHAM

TROUBLE with LICHEN

Introduction by Kate Folk

THE MODERN LIBRARY

NEW YORK

2022 Modern Library Trade Paperback Edition

Copyright © 1960 by John Wyndham
Copyright renewed 1988 by Isabel Grace Harris
Introduction copyright © 2022 by Kate Folk

Published in the United States by The Modern Library, an
imprint of Random House, a division of Penguin Random
House LLC, New York.

Originally published in hardcover in the United Kingdom by
Michael Joseph, an imprint of Penguin Random House UK,
and in paperback in the United States by Ballantine Books,
an imprint of Random House, a division of
Penguin Random House LLC, in 1960.

ISBN 978-0-593-45014-7
Ebook ISBN 978-0-593-45015-4

Printed in the United States of America on acid-free paper

modernlibrary.com
randomhousebooks.com

1st Printing

CONTENTS

INTRODUCTION

Kate Folk

Trouble with Lichen opens with a funeral. Hundreds of women (along with a "sprinkling" of men) have turned out to mourn the book's heroine, Diana Brackley. She's beloved by these women, we'll learn, for prolonging their lives, freeing them from having to choose between a family and a career outside the home. Two decades before Helen Gurley Brown's self-help book *Having It All* and Enjoli's iconic "eight-hour perfume for the twenty-four-hour woman" advert, John Wyndham posited that the only way a woman could have it all was to extend her life to two hundred years.

Wyndham's preferred genre was what he called "logical fantasy," in which a sci-fi premise is imposed on an otherwise recognizable version of society, and allowed to play out as it might in the real world. Logical fantasy describes *Lichen* aptly. Wyndham shows how a discovery that seems, on its face, to be an unmitigated triumph—a form of lichen that dramatically slows the aging process—would become fodder for ongoing political and cultural battles. Snippets of newspaper articles, each applying their own spin to what the "antigerone" means for society, are the precursor of endless Twitter discourses. The convoluted ways in which different parties distort a scientific advancement to fit their agendas feels too real in 2022. Before the pandemic, I wouldn't have imagined that ostensibly benign public health tools like masks and vaccines would be so polarizing, but I'm willing to bet that Wyndham would have seen it coming.

The heart of *Lichen* is Diana, a protagonist who remains a bit of a cipher throughout the book. As another character says of her, Diana "has a way of smiling at the wrong things," one of my favorite lines. After the opening funeral scene, we shift backward in time to meet Diana as she's graduating from secondary school. She dreams of a career beyond what she calls "one of the dead-end jobs" of "being just a woman and nothing else." This streak of defiance makes her parents nervous, and to their chagrin, Diana's ambition proves more than a phase. She reads biochemistry at Cambridge, and after graduating, she lands a job at Darr House Developments, where she meets her mentor and love interest, Francis Saxover. In an accident of fate, Diana leaves a saucer of milk out overnight, and in the morning she and Francis find that part of the milk hasn't turned—the part that was touching remnants of a lichen specimen. After experimenting separately, they both conclude that this lichen, which Francis calls lichenin, slows the aging process. Depending on the dosage given, it can prolong human life to two or even three hundred years.

Wyndham rarely allows us a glimpse of Diana's interior life. Instead, her thoughts are revealed through dialogue, action, and the observations of other characters. As a beautiful young woman who's apparently uninterested in marriage, Diana is the object of constant scrutiny. She seems unbothered by this, however, too focused on grander goals to worry about other people's gossip. Diana believes that "the greatest enemies of women aren't men at all, they are women: silly women, lazy women, and smug women." At times, the book's contempt for "silly women" feels like it's joining in on the misogyny rather than critiquing it. I suspect Wyndham held the same prejudice as his supporting characters, which sorts women into one of two buckets: brilliant women who commit themselves to a vocation, and ordinary women who conform to the "easy" role of wife and mother. This formulation doesn't allow for the possibility of a mother being anything but a mindless drone, incapable of ambition beyond child-rearing. But, in spite of some clumsy moments, and perhaps sometimes unintentionally, Wyndham vividly demonstrates how his contemporaries attempted to control women by boxing them into types, and punishing them when they displayed signs of greater complexity.

It was a genius move for Wyndham to center an age-slowing narrative on women, who are still today pressured to remain youthful-looking forever, or succumb to social invisibility. Men and women both fear death, Diana says, but "a man is not so constantly haunted by thoughts of time and age as a woman is." "A woman is always up against time," as Diana's mother reminds her. Diana's plot for overthrowing this order involves starting a beauty company whose products promise to "preserve your youth," a common refrain in that industry. It's to Diana's advantage that her clients take this promise seriously, but not literally. "Miracle is a favorite word in women's papers," she says. "Nobody seriously expects it to *mean* anything." This reminds me of how online reviewers will declare a product the "holy grail" of serums or chemical exfoliators. The fact that cosmetic products are routinely described in quasi-religious terms points to how high the stakes are for women to maintain a youthful appearance.

Diana's plot goes beyond the advancement of women, however. She believes that, given a longer lifespan, people will become better equipped to solve the existential crises facing humanity. Diana could be referencing climate change when she describes humanity's "drift" toward catastrophe, which we allow "with an evil irresponsibility, because with our ordinary short lives we shan't be here to see it." Diana believes that if people live longer, they will, as a matter of course, develop into wiser, more virtuous individuals. The world's "clever moneymakers," she claims, will grow bored of accumulating wealth for its own sake, and instead "turn their cleverness to something more useful." I was skeptical of this aspect of Diana's theory, which has the facile logic of trickle-down economics. It seems likelier that an antigerone, being presumably rare and expensive, would bolster social Darwinist views of the rich as biologically superior to the poor, providing a sinister new gloss of justification for inequality.

In the book, representatives of the working class advance a different objection to lichenin, claiming it will be used to further exploit their labor. One protestor deems the antigerone "the dirtiest weapon of all the dirty weapons that the Tories have aimed at the workers," going on to explain that it will mean "working for *three* lifetimes instead of one." It's true that for Diana, and the upper-class women she enlists in her "corps" fighting on behalf of the antigerone, a longer life means a chance to become self-actualized, whereas for less privileged women, it could mean something very different. The book seems to regard these objections as alarmist and a bit silly, though I wondered if they had a point. Fed into the capitalist machine, a scientific advancement will inevitably be used to maximize profits, regardless of the human toll. Rather than transforming society, new technologies usually just accelerate existing trends. I shudder to think of what "rise and grind" influencers would make of lichenin. Imagine the podcast ads!

Unusual for his time, and especially for the work of male sci-fi writers, Wyndham's novels were notable for their strong female characters. Perhaps due to his parents' tumultuous relationship, Wyndham was leery of pursuing marriage and family. In her illuminating biography *Hidden Wyndham*, Amy Binns posits that Wyndham was repelled by what he viewed as his mother's "passive dependency" on men. Wyndham believed that marriage "diminished women into little more than brainwashed slaves" (Binns). Wyndham's lifelong partner, Grace Wilson, was the opposite of this stereotype. Wilson worked as a schoolteacher, which she considered her life's calling. Like Wyndham, she didn't consider marriage a priority. For thirty years, the two resided in separate rooms at the Penn Club, a no-frills hotel in Bloomsbury, the heart of London's literary scene. When they became romantically involved, in 1935, a "marriage bar" forced women teachers to stop working if they married, and so Wyndham and Wilson kept their relationship secret. But even after the bar was lifted in 1938, Wyndham and Wilson maintained a secret relationship for decades, until finally marrying in 1963, six years before Wyndham's death. This furtiveness wasn't unusual for Wyndham, who was the subject of a 2005 BBC documentary subtitled *The Invisible Man of Science Fiction,* and Wilson also seemed content with the arrangement. I admire how they staked out a partnership on their own terms, one that was apparently built upon equality and mutual respect. As I read *Lichen,* I couldn't help but see Grace Wilson's imprint on the character of Diana.

The book's themes ring true in 2022, as I'm writing this, in ways both cathartic and horrifying. Maybe Diana is right, and if our politicians and billionaires knew they'd be alive to witness the worst of the climate catastrophe, they'd feel compelled to invest in real mitigation efforts, even if it meant a short-term hit to their financial portfolios. Then again, maybe they'd merely use the extra years to build luxury underground bunkers for their families, or further their harebrained schemes to colonize space. Wyndham was uniquely gifted at skewering humankind's foibles while maintaining a shred of hope that our better angels would prevail. I wish lichenin were real if only so that Wyndham could be alive today, a spry 118-year-old, to apply his logical fantasy treatment to our bonkers current moment.

———

KATE FOLK is the author of *Out There,* a story collection (Random House, 2022). She's the recipient of a Stegner Fellowship in fiction from Stanford University, and has written for publications including *The New Yorker, The New York Times Magazine, Granta, McSweeney's Quarterly Concern,* and *Zyzzyva.* She lives in San Francisco.

TROUBLE with LICHEN

PROLOGUE

The farewell was beautiful.

The small choir, all in white, with gold nets gleaming on its hair, sang with the sweet sadness of angels forlorn.

When it finished, the crowded chapel was full of absolute silence, and through the heavy air the scent of thousands of flowers rolled in slow waves.

The coffin topped a small pyramid of close-packed blooms. At the four corners, guards in classical gowns of purple silk, gold nets on their bowed heads, gold cords crossing between their breasts, each with a gilded palm frond in her hand, stood as if carved.

The bishop crossed the floor soundlessly to ascend the four steps to the low pulpit. He laid his book carefully on the shelf before him, paused, and looked up.

". . . our beloved sister, Diana . . . her unfinished work which she now can never finish . . . irony of fate not a proper term to apply to the will of the Lord . . . He giveth; He taketh away . . . if He takes away the olive tree He has given before its fruit has ripened, it is for us to accept His will . . . Vessel of His inspiration . . . Devotion to her aims . . . Fortitude . . . Change in the course of human history . . . The body of Thy servant, Diana. . . ."

The eyes of the congregation, the several hundred women with a sprinkling of men, turned to the coffin. Slowly, it started to move. A few disturbed blossoms rolled down and spilled upon the carpet. Inexorably the coffin slid on. The organ began to play softly. The voices of the choir rose again, high and clear. The curtains dragged along the sides of the coffin, and fell to behind it.

There was a sound of caught breaths, a whimper or two, a dappling of small white handkerchiefs...

As they left, Zephanie and Richard became separated from her father. She turned, and saw him a few yards behind them. Among the press of women in the aisle he seemed taller than he was. His handsome face told nothing. It looked only tired—and unconscious of everything about him.

Outside, there were more women; hundreds of them who had not been able to get into the chapel. Many were weeping. The flowers they had brought were laid like a bright carpet on either side of the door so that those leaving had to walk between them. Someone in the crowd was holding a pole that bore a large *crux ansata*. It was made entirely of arum lilies, and crossed by a broad, black silk ribbon.

On the gravel, Zephanie towed Richard clear of the stream, and stood looking at the scene. Her own eyes were moist, but, for all that, a rueful smile touched the corners of her mouth.

"Poor darling Diana," she said. "Just think how this would have amused her."

She produced her own handkerchief to pat it at her eyes briefly. Then, in a brisk tone, she said:

"Come on. Let's find Daddy, and get him out of this."

But it was a lovely funeral.

—

The *News-Record* reported:

> ... Women in all walks of life, from every corner of Britain had gathered to pay their last respects. Many arrived soon after dawn to join those who had camped all night outside the cemetery gates.

When at last the long vigil was rewarded by the arrival of the slow, flowers-laden procession, the spectators pressed forward against the restraining ranks of the police, many strewing flowers before the wheels. As the cortège passed tears streamed down the faces of the mourners, and sounds of ululation* broke from the patient ranks.

Not since the funeral of Emily Davison† has London witnessed such a tribute to a woman by women.

—

And then, because the *News-Record* is always anxious that its readers shall understand what it has written, there were two footnotes:

* ululation—a wailing, or howling.
† The funeral of Emily Wilding Davison took place June 14, 1913. She was a member of the Women's Suffrage movement who died as a result of injuries received when she threw herself in front of the King's horse during the Derby, run on June 4 that year.

Part ONE

1

The floor of the hall had been cleared. Someone had put rather somber bunches of evergreens here and there on the walls. Somebody else had thought a little tinsel might cheer them up. The tables, set end to end down one side, made a white-clothed counter supporting plates of sandwiches, plates of bright cakes, some dishes of sausage-rolls, jugs of lemon, jugs of orange, vases of flowers, and, intermittently, urns. To the eye, the rest of the room suggested a palette in motion. For the ear, even from a little way off, there was a reminder of starlings at dusk.

St. Merryn's High was holding its end-of-term party.

Miss Benbow, maths, while listening to a tedious account of the intelligence shown by Aurora Tregg's puppy, let her gaze wander round the room, noting those she must have a word with in the course of the evening. Up at the far end she saw Diana Brackley, alone for the moment. Diana was certainly one who deserved congratulations, so, seizing a pause in Aurora's breathless delivery, she commended the puppy's sagacity, wished it well in the future, and broke away.

Crossing the room she had a sudden glimpse of Diana through a stranger's eyes: no longer a schoolgirl, but an attractive young woman. Perhaps it was the dress that did it. A simple navy-blue face-cloth, unnoticeable among the rest until you really looked at it. It had been inexpensive—Miss Benbow knew that it must have been—yet there was a quality of style about it, or was there really? She wasn't quite sure. Diana had taste in clothes, and that something else that can make three guineas look like twenty. A gift, Miss Benbow thought ruefully, not to be despised. And, she went on, still seeing through the new refraction, the looks were a part of the gift. Not pretty. Pretty girls are lovely as the flowers in May, but there are so many flowers in May. No one who knew words could call Diana pretty . . .

Eighteen—just eighteen—Diana was then. Fairly tall—five foot ten, or thereabouts—and slender, and straight. Her hair was a dark chestnut, with a glint of russet lights. The line of her forehead and nose was not truly Grecian, yet it had a classic quality. Her mouth was a little reddened, for one must not go to a party undressed, but, in contrast with the many rosebuds and gashes to be seen all around, she had just the quantity and the color that suited the occasion. The mouth itself had a kind of formally decorative appearance which told one practically nothing—yet it could smile with charm on occasion, and did not do it too often. But at closer range it was her gray eyes one noticed, and was aware of all the time; not only because they were fine eyes, beautifully spaced and set, but even more on account of their steadiness, the unembarrassed calmness with which they took in, and considered. With a kind of surprise, because she was in the habit of thinking of her as a mind rather than as a shape, Miss Benbow realized that Diana had become what in the youth of her parents' generation would have been termed "a beauty."

This thought was immediately followed by a pleasant sense of self-congratulation, for in a school like St. Merryn's High you not only teach and attempt to educate a child; you conduct a kind of jungle warfare on her behalf—and the better-looking the child, the more slender, generally speaking, are her chances of survival, for the partisans of ignorance enfilade your route in greater numbers.

The touts for dead-end jobs slink along beside you, butterflies with wings of iridescent bank-notes flutter just within reach tempting your charge to chase them, the miasma of the picture-papers taints the air, the sticky webs of early marriage are spun close by the track, hen-witted mothers dart suddenly out of the bushes, myopic fathers blunder uncertainly onto the path; rectangular, flickering eyes gleam hypnotically from the shadows, tomtoms beat a restless, moonstruck rhythm, and up above there are the mocking-birds, always crying: "What does it matter as long as she's happy . . . ? What does it matter . . . ? What does it matter . . . ?"

So you are entitled, surely, to feel some pride of achievement when you regard those whom you have helped to guide past these perils.

But then, in honesty, Miss Benbow had to call herself to order for taking unearned credit. Diana, one must admit, had required little protection. The hazards did not trouble her. The temptations she regarded aloofly, as if it had never crossed her mind that they were intended to tempt *her*. Hers was something the manner of an intelligent traveler passing through interesting country. Her destination might be unknown as yet, but it was certainly ahead, and that anyone should be satisfied to drop off this early at wayside halts and primitive villages simply puzzled her. No, one was glad Diana had done so well, but one must not take too much credit for it. She had worked hard and deserved her success—the only thing was that one could have wished—although it did seem a rather dreadful thing to wish when one had to strive so hard with inertly conformist children—but one did wish that she were perhaps a little less, well—individual . . . ?

By this time Miss Benbow was near the end of her room, and Diana had seen her approaching.

"Good evening, Miss Benbow."

"Good evening, Diana. I did so want to congratulate you. It's splendid, perfectly splendid. Mind you, we all knew you'd do well—we should have been dreadfully disappointed if it had been anything less than well. But this—well, it's better than I dared to hope for you."

"Thank you so much, Miss Benbow. But it wasn't all me. I mean, I wouldn't have got very far without all of you helping me and telling me *what* to do, would I?"

"That's what we're here for, but we are in debt to you, too, Diana. Even in these days a scholarship brings credit to a school—and yours is one of the best St. Merryn's has ever gained. I expect you know that."

"Miss Fortindale did seem really pleased about it."

"She's more than pleased, Diana. She's delighted. We all are."

"Thank you, Miss Benbow."

"And, of course, your parents must be delighted, too."

"Yes," agreed Diana, with a touch of reservation. "Daddy's very pleased. He likes the idea of Cambridge for me because he's always wished that he'd been able to go there himself. If I'd failed the scholarship Cambridge would have been out of the question: it would have had to be just—" in the nick of time she remembered that Miss Benbow was a graduate of London, and amended to "—one of the redbricks."

"Some of the redbricks are doing very good work," Miss Benbow said, with a faint touch of reproof.

"Oh, yes, of course. It's only that when you've made up your mind to do something—well, having to do something else *is* a kind of failure, however you look at it, isn't it?"

Miss Benbow resisted being drawn along that line.

"And your mother? She must be very proud of your success, too."

Diana looked at her with those gray eyes that seemed to see further back into one's head than most people's.

"Yes," she said, judicially, "that's how Mummy feels about it."

Miss Benbow's eyebrows rose slightly.

"I mean, that she must be very proud of my success," Diana explained.

"But, surely, she *is*," protested Miss Benbow.

"She tries. She's really been awfully sweet about it," said Diana. She fixed Miss Benbow with those eyes again. "Why is it that mothers still think it so much more respectable to be bed-worthy than brainy?" she inquired. "I mean, you'd expect it to be the other way round."

Miss Benbow blinked. Something awkward was bound to crop up in conversation with Diana, but she took it straight.

"I think," she said judicially, "that I would substitute 'compre-hensible' for 'respectable.' After all, the 'brainy' world is a mys-terious closed book to the majority of mothers so they feel uncertain about it; but they are all, rather naturally, under the impression that they are authorities on the other, so that they can understand, and help."

Diana considered.

"But 'respectable' does come into it somehow—though I don't quite see why," she said, with a slight frown.

Miss Benbow gave a slight shake of her head.

"Aren't you mixing up respectability and conformity?" she asked. "It's natural for parents to want children to conform to a pattern they understand." She hesitated, and then went on: "Has it ever occurred to you that when the daughter of a domestic-minded woman chooses to have a career she is criticizing her mother by implication? She is saying, in effect: 'The kind of life that was good enough for you, Mother, isn't good enough for me.' Well, mothers—like other people—don't care for that very much."

"I hadn't looked at it that way before," Diana admitted thoughtfully. "You mean that, underneath, they are always hop-ing that their daughters will fail in their careers, and so prove that they, the mothers, I mean, were right all the time?"

"You do dash off, don't you, Diana?"

"But—well, it does follow, doesn't it, Miss Benbow?"

"I don't think we'll do any more following at the moment. Where are you going for your holidays, Diana?"

"Germany," Diana told her. "I'd rather go to France really, but Germany seems to be more useful."

They chatted about that for a time. Then Miss Benbow congratulated her again, and wished her well in her university life.

"I'm terribly grateful for everything. And I'm so glad *you're* all so pleased," Diana told her. "It's a funny thing," she added meditatively, "I should have thought practically *anybody* could be bedworthy, if she put her mind to it—I mean, even if she hadn't much mind to put. So I don't see why—"

But Miss Benbow declined to be re-entangled.

"Oh!" she exclaimed, "there's Miss Taplow. I know she's anxious to have a few words with you. Come along."

She managed the transfer efficiently, and as Miss Taplow began, a little warily, to congratulate Diana, Miss Benbow turned to find herself face to face with Brenda Watkins. As she felicitated Brenda whose very small, very new engagement ring obviously ranked above all possible scholarships in every university, she could hear Diana's voice behind her saying:

"Well, being just a woman and nothing else does strike me as one of the dead-end jobs, Miss Taplow. I mean you can't get any promotion in it, can you?—well, not unless you take it up as a courtesan, or something . . ."

———

"I simply don't understand where she gets it from," said Mrs. Brackley, with a perplexed expression.

"Well, it wasn't from me," her husband told her. "I've sometimes wished a bit of braininess did run in our family, but, as far as I know, it never has. Anyway, I can't see that it matters very much where it came from."

"It wasn't really the braininess I was thinking about. Father must have had brains of a kind, or he'd not have done so well in the contracting business. No, it's this—well, I suppose you could call it independence . . . the way she keeps on questioning things. Things that don't *need* questioning."

"And finding some pretty funny answers from what I've heard now and then," Mr. Brackley said.

"It's a kind of restlessness," Malvina Brackley persisted. "Of course, young girls *do* get restless—one expects it, but—well, I mean, this isn't the usual way."

"No boy-friends," her husband observed bluntly. "No good wanting trouble, my dear. It'll come."

"But it would be more normal. A good-looking girl like Diana . . ."

"She could have boy-friends if she wanted to. She's only got to learn to giggle, and not say things that panic them."

"Oh, Diana's not a prig, Harold."

"I know she's not. But they think she is. Very conventional neighborhood this. Three kinds of girls: 'sports,' gigglers, and prigs, no others recognized. It's bad enough to have to live in an uncivilized area; surely you don't *want* her to take up with any of its oafs?"

"No, no of course not. It's just that . . ."

"I know. It'd be more *normal*. My dear, last time we talked to Miss Pattison at the school she predicted a brilliant future for Diana. Brilliant was the word, and it doesn't mean normal. You can't have it both ways."

"It's more important for her to be happy than brilliant."

"My dear, you're getting very close to suggesting that all what you call normal people are happy people. And that is one hell of a proposition. Just look at 'em . . . No, let's be thankful, very thankful, that she hasn't fallen for any of the oafs. There'd be no brilliant future for her there—nor, come to think of it, for the oaf. Don't you worry. She'll find her own way. What she needs is more scope."

"Of course, there was my mother's youngest sister, my Aunt Annie," Mrs. Brackley said, thoughtfully. "She wasn't quite ordinary."

"Why, what was wrong with her?"

"Oh, I don't mean that way. No, she went to prison in 1912—or was it 1913?—for letting off fire-crackers in Piccadilly."

"What on earth did she do that for?"

"She threw them in among the horses' legs and caused such a tangle that the traffic was jammed from Bond Street to Swan and Edgar's, and then she climbed on top of a bus and shouted 'Votes for Women' till they took her away. She got a month for that. The family was very ashamed.

"Soon after she came out she threw a brick through a window in Oxford Street, and got two months. She wasn't very well when she came out after that because she hunger-struck, so my grandmother took her down to the country. But she got back somehow, and succeeded in throwing a bottle of ink over Mr. Balfour, so they took her off again, and this time she very nearly set a wing of Holloway prison on fire."

"An enterprising woman, your aunt. But I don't quite see . . . ?"

"Well, *she* wasn't just an ordinary person. So Diana may get it from my mother's family."

"I'm not sure what it is that Diana may have got from a militant great-aunt, and frankly, my dear, I don't give a hoot where it came from, beyond the fact that whatever she has, we have somehow transmitted to her between us. And I think we've done a good, if rather astonishing, job."

"Of course we have, Harold, dear. We've every right to be proud of her. It's only—well, it's not always the most brilliant life that's the happiest, is it?"

"I don't know. You and I know—at least I know—that one can

be happy without being brilliant—what it feels like to be brilliant, and what you want then to make you happy I haven't a clue. But I do know that it can make someone else happy. Me, for one thing—and for a thoroughly selfish reason. Ever since she was a little girl it's been on my conscience that I couldn't afford to send her to a first-class school—oh, I know the St. Merryn's people are good teachers, she's proved that, but it's not the same. When your father died I thought we might be able to manage it. I went to the solicitors, and put it to them. They were sorry, but firm. The instructions were quite clear, they said. The money is in trust until she is twenty-five. It cannot be touched, nor may anything be raised on it, even for her education."

"You never told me about that, Harold."

"There wasn't much point in telling either of you until I knew whether it could be done. And it couldn't. You know, Malvina, I think that was about the shabbiest of all the things your father did to us. Leaving you nothing—well, that was just in character. But to leave our daughter forty thousand pounds, and then tie it up so that in the most critical formative years of her life she could have no benefit from it . . . ! So I say, good for Diana. She's done for herself what I couldn't do for her, and what he wouldn't do for her. She's wiped the old bastard's eye properly, without even knowing it."

"Harold, dear—!"

"I know, my dear, I know. But really . . . ! I don't think of the malignant old so-and-so much these days, but when I do . . ." He broke off. He looked round the small sitting-room. That wasn't too bad; a bit shabby now, but comfortable. But the mean little semi-detached house set in a street of exactly similar houses in this seedy suburb . . . The narrow life . . . The struggle to get along on a salary which always lagged behind prices . . . So few of the things Malvina must long for, and ought to have had . . .

"Still no regrets?" he asked her.

She smiled back.

"None, darling. None at all."

He picked her up, and went back to the armchair with her. She laid her head on his shoulder.

"None," she said quietly. Then she added: "*I* shouldn't have been any happier for winning scholarships."

"Darling, people aren't all alike. I'm coming to the conclusion we're a bit exceptional, anyway. How many of the people you know in this road could truthfully say 'no regrets'?"

"There must be some."

"I rather think it doesn't often happen. And however much you wish it for other people you certainly can't make it happen. What's more, Diana isn't much like you—she isn't much like me, either. Goodness knows who she is like. So it's no good worrying because she doesn't want to do what you would want to do if you were in her place—and *if* you could recall just what it feels like to be eighteen. Brilliant, they said. Well, the only thing we can do is to watch our daughter being brilliant in her own way—and back her up, of course."

"Harold, she doesn't know about the money, does she?"

"She knows there is some money, of course. She didn't ask how much. I didn't have to lie. I just tried to give the impression of—well nothing very much, say three or four hundred pounds. It seemed wiser."

"I'm sure it is. I'll remember that, if she mentions it."

After a pause, she inquired:

"Harold, I expect it sounds very stupid of me, but what does a chemist actually *do*? I mean, Diana has explained that it's not the same as a pharmacist, and I was glad about that, but she didn't make it very clear."

"Nor am I, my dear. I should think we'd better ask her again. Yes. The see-saw has tipped, all right—we've reached the stage where *she* tells *us*."

—

It turned out not to matter much to the Brackleys what a chemist did do, for in the course of her first year Diana changed her mind, deciding to read biochemistry instead, and what a biochemist did was something that her mother never did succeed in getting clear in her mind.

The reason for this change lay somewhere in a lecture given before the Mid-Twentieth Society on *Some Evolutionary Trends in Recently Modified Environments.* It did not sound very exciting, and Diana was never quite sure how it was that she had come to attend it. Nevertheless, she did, and, in doing so, took a step which was to determine the course of her life.

The speaker was Francis Saxover, Sc.D., F.R.S., sometime Gilkes Professor of Biochemistry in the University of Cambridge, and widely regarded as an intellectual renegade. He came of a South Staffordshire family which, after potting in a small way for unrecorded generations, had, about the middle of the eighteenth century, acquired a notable gene of enterprise. This gene, so suited to the climate of the time and to the imminent industrial age, had led the Saxovers into new methods of firing, applications of steam power, reorganization of production, and so, by taking advantage of the new navigation canals, to a world-wide trade, and a large family fortune.

Nor had it weakened in the succeeding generations. There was no clogs-to-clogs about the Saxovers. They kept in the van with new processes and methods, and even went into plastics when they perceived in them a growing competitor for crocks. In the second half of the twentieth century they were still doing well.

In Francis, however, the spirit of enterprise had taken a different course. He had been content to leave the family concerns in the hands of his two elder brothers and follow his own bent to its culmination in a Chair. Or so he thought.

It had happened, however, that the health of Joseph Saxover, his father, had become uncertain in his later middle-life. Upon discovering this, Joseph, a provident man, had lost no time in making over his holdings and putting his two elder sons in full charge of the business. He had then devoted much time in the remaining eight or nine years of his life to the fascinating hobby of devising schemes to defeat the rapacity of the Exchequer. Certain scruples prevented him from doing quite as well in this field as some of his competitors, but he, nevertheless, did well enough to set the authorities blocking a number of interesting lacunae against imitators after his death.

As a result of the maneuvers Francis had found himself a great deal better off than he had expected to be, and became disturbed. It was as if that Saxover gene had been pricked into activity by the thought of capital unemployed. After an increasingly restless year he had resigned his Chair, and removed himself from the cloister to do battle in the market-place.

With a few trustful assistants he had set up a research establishment of his own, and set out to justify his contention that discovery, in spite of popular opinion, was still not exclusively the province of massed researchers working for huge companies in semi-military formations.

Darr House Developments, as the company was known, simply from the title of the estate he had bought for it, had at that time been in operation for six years. Not only was that five years longer than most of his friends had predicted, but it appeared to have made a promising start. Already it held several patents important enough to have roused interest among the larger chemical manufacturers: and, perhaps, a little envy among former colleagues. Certainly there was a tinge of malice in the suggestion that this visit of Francis's to his former haunts sprang less from his desire to instruct than from his company's need to recruit.

Oddly enough, Diana could never recall the lecture in any detail. Quite early on, she remembered, he had stated, more as though it were a self-evident fact than a proposition, that the dominant figure of yesterday was the engineer; of today, the physicist; of tomorrow, the biochemist. Once this thought had been presented to Diana, she could not imagine why she had not perceived it before. Stirred as if by a revelation, she had a quite overwhelming sense of understanding, for the first time, the meaning of the word "vocation." Whereafter, she hung upon the lecturer's words—at least, she had the impression she was hanging upon them, though it was a bit puzzling that she could never recall any of them, and that they seemed to have fused into an *en bloc* support for the sense of vocation.

Francis Saxover was then still under forty. A spare man with an aquiline face, who gave the impression of being a little over, rather than half an inch under, six feet. His hair was still dark except for a little graying at the sides. His eyebrows, while not bushy, contrived nevertheless to bristle forward, slightly shadowing his eyes and giving them an appearance of being more deeply set than they were. His manner was easy and relaxed, he talked rather than lectured, roving his platform lankily, and using his brown, long-fingered hands to emphasize his points.

All that Diana really took away from the lecture was a mental picture of the lecturer, a strong impression of his purposeful enthusiasm—and, of course, the sense of having discovered the only life-work worthwhile....

And so, the change of school to biochemistry.

And so, a lot of hard work.

And so, in due course, an Honours Degree.

And then, the question of a job.

Diana suggested Darr House Developments. This was not immediately acclaimed.

"H'm. Possible, on your showing," admitted her tutor. "But

Saxover's pretty choosey. Can afford to be on what he pays, of course, but the turnover of staff is said to be a bit high there. Why don't you consider one of the big firms? Plenty of scope, more stability, not spectacular as a rule, I grant you, but it's good solid work that counts in the end."

But Diana favored Darr House.

"I'd like to try there," she said firmly. "If it isn't a success, I can try one of the big companies later on, but from what I hear it would very likely be more difficult the other way round."

"Very well," said her tutor, and her manner relaxed slightly. "As a matter of fact," she confided, "at your age I'd feel the same. It's parents who don't."

"Mine won't mind," Diana told her. "If I were a son, they'd probably want me to go into one of the big companies, but girls are different. Their serious interests are only a frivolous preliminary to taking up the frivolous life seriously, so it isn't thought to matter much, you see."

"See is a rather definite word for that, but I perceive the drift," her tutor said. "All right. Then I'll drop a line to Saxover for you. It could be interesting there, I think. Incidentally, did you see that he's now produced a virus that produces sterility in the male locust?—Admittedly the female locust can go on producing female locusts for a number of generations without male assistance, but one feels that it must tell sooner or later, or there wouldn't be much sense in sex, would there . . . ?"

—

"Of course I hope you get the job if it's what you want, darling, but what *is* this Darr House place?"

"It's a research center. A company, but a private one run by a Dr. Saxover, Mummy. There's a big late-eighteenth-century house in a park. One of those places that's too big for anybody to live in, but not interesting enough for the National Trust. Dr. Saxover bought it nearly ten years ago. He and his family live in a wing of the house. The rest has been turned into offices and labs, and so on. The coach-houses and stables were converted into flatlets for the staff. And there are several cottages on the estate. And after a bit he built more labs, and some new houses for the married staff, and so on. It's a sort of community."

"You'd have to live there?"

"Yes—or nearby. Somebody told me it has overflowed a bit, but if I were lucky I might get one of the flatlets. There's a sort of staff dining-hall in the house you can use if you like. And, of course, one can get away at weekends. Everybody says it's a lovely place, right in the country. But you do have to work, and you have to be interested. He doesn't want time-servers."

Mrs. Brackley said:

"It sounds a very nice place, I'm sure, darling, but we don't know much about this kind of thing, your father and I. What's puzzling us is what does this place really do? What do they make there?"

"They don't actually *make* anything, Mummy. They work out ideas, and then license other people to use them."

"But if they're good ideas, why don't they use them themselves?"

"That isn't their job. Darr House isn't a factory, you see. What happens is—well, as an example, Dr. Saxover had an idea about termites—white ants, you know—they eat houses and things all over the tropics—"

"Houses, darling?"

"Well, the wooden parts, and then the rest falls down. So Dr. Saxover and the Darr House people went into it. Now, a termite chews up wood and swallows it, but by itself it can't digest it any more than we could, but there is a protozoan parasite living inside the termite which breaks down the cellulose structure of the wood, and then the termite *can* digest it, and live on it. So the Darr House people investigated the parasite, and looked for a chemical compound that would be fatal to it. Well, they found one that was effective and safe to use. They gave it to termites, the termites went on chewing wood, but without the parasite they couldn't digest it, so they just starved and died.

"So the Darr House people called this stuff AP-91 and patented it, and Dr. Saxover took it to Commonwealth Chemical Enterprises, and suggested that there would be a big tropical market for it. C.C.E. tested it, and found it satisfactory, so they agreed to manufacture it. And now they sell it all over the tropics under the trade name of Termorb-6, and Dr. Saxover collects a royalty on every tin they sell. That alone must bring in thousands a year, and there are quite a lot of other patents as well. That's roughly the way it works."

"White ants. How horrid!" said Mrs. Brackley. "I shouldn't like to work on ants."

"That was only one project, Mummy. There are several going at a time on lots of different things."

"This place. Are there many there?"

"I don't know quite how many. Somewhere about sixty, I think."

"Are many of them girls?"

"Yes, darling. The decencies are preserved, too. I'm told that the incidence of marriage is quite high. Though I'm not quite sure whether you'd consider that for or against. However, not to worry, I haven't the least intention of joining the great majority yet awhile."

"Darling, that expression is usually used to mean—"

"I know, Mummy. I know—oh, you've not seen the new dress I've got for the interview yet. Come up and I'll show you . . ."

2

Diana never knew it, but the new dress came near to losing her the job. Not that there was anything wrong with it; on the contrary. It was made of a thin woollen material in a soft green which became her chestnut hair well, and, as did most of her clothes, looked worth quite a little more than its price. But, while there is no uniform for young scientists comparable with that which indicates some kind of association with art, they do tend in general to divide into two main types; the not-very-well-cut neat-presentable, and the scruffy, and Diana was decidedly neither. The sight of her caused Francis Saxover misgivings.

Her qualifications had satisfied him, her references and recommendations were good, her own letter of application had impressed him very favorably. Indeed, it could be said that all the signals were set in her favor until her arrival qualified them by setting up an amber.

For, in his near ten years now of managing Darr House Developments, Francis had grown a little cagey. He had fully intended to be, as he was, the inspiration and direction of his venture; what he had failed to foresee, however, was that he would be forced by circumstances to become to some extent the patriarch of the community that he had brought together. This imposition had led him to regard candidates with a split eye, and it was the patriarchal half that now viewed the personable and decorative Miss Brackley with dubiety.

She looked eminently capable of provoking another of those situations which had set him wondering audibly to Caroline, his wife, whether they had not better change the word "Developments" to "Holiday Camp and Lonely Hearts Bureau."

Diana herself was puzzled to know why, after good auguries and a promising start, the interview seemed to go less well. The situation would have been clearer to her had she been able to glimpse some of the precedents that were flitting through her prospective employer's mind. He was recalling less striking persons than Diana who had turned out to be sherbet powder in the waters of his peaceful community.

The sloe-eyed, somewhat sultry Miss Tregarven, for instance. She had been a biologist of promise, but unfortunately she was also a girl whose room decorations had included a row of small china hearts which she ceremoniously cracked one by one with a special little hammer as circumstances seemed to her to justify raising the score. And, too, there had been Miss Blew, a doll-like creature with an undoubted touch of chemic genius, and an entirely misleading expression of seraphic innocence fraught with great Galahad-rousing power. The widespread desire to be of service to Miss Blew had eventually reached its highest manifestation in a duel—an inexpert contest, staged one dewy dawn in the meadow beside the woods, between a chemist and a biologist, in the course of which the chemist had run the biologist through the left arm, thus enraging the biologist who had then abandoned his weapon in order to knock the chemist out with an honest fist, and Miss Blew, who had sneaked out, straight from bed and mistily clad, to watch the fray from the cover of some bushes, took a severe chill. Also, Miss Cotch. Miss Cotch had been a dab at handling the amino-acids, but less adept at managing her own affairs, being under the handicap of an excessively tender heart. Indeed, so averse was she from hurting anyone's feelings that she had somehow managed to get herself secretly engaged to three of her fellow-workers at the same time, and then, perceiving no way out of this impasse but flight, had disappeared, leaving a welter of emotional and departmental disorder behind her.

In view of these and several other such experiences Francis's hesitation was not unjustified. On the other hand, and in Diana's favor, he noted that she was taking the interview absolutely straight, depending on her merits, and making no attempt to charm herself into the job. Out of fairness he decided it was a case for a second opinion—for, after all, Caroline also was sometimes called upon to dress the emotional wounds caused by these affairs—so, instead of introducing Diana to the staff dining-room, as he had intended, he invited her to luncheon in the private wing.

Over the meal his misgivings receded. She talked easily and intelligently to her host and hostess, exchanged some thoughts with Paul, who was then twelve, upon the probable date of a successful Martian expedition, and did her best to get a few words out of Zephanie, who regarded her with round-eyed awe, and was struck almost dumb with admiration.

Afterward, he put it to Caroline.

"Do we risk it, or should we be asking for more trouble?"

Caroline had looked at him sadly.

"Francis, dear, you really must stop burdening yourself with the idea that the place could, or should, run like a machine. It never will."

"I'm beginning to understand that," Francis admitted. "All the same, there's a difference between facing routine crises, and acting in a way that will produce better ones."

"Well, if you think that putting your applicants through a kind of beauty competition in reverse is going to do anything more than encourage the less-favored to get above themselves and try *their* strength, you'd better reconsider. I like the girl. She's unusual. She's intelligent—and I rather think she's got good sense, which is not the same thing. So, if she has the knowledge and ability you need, then let her come."

Diana got the job, and joined the staff of Darr.

Her arrival aroused considerable interest, both hopeful and wary. The quick-off-the-mark types tried their luck forthwith, and found no encouragement. The subtler strategists went to work, and somehow bogged down at quite an early stage. With these preliminaries as a guide, Darr began to make up its mind about her.

"Beautiful but dumb," one of the chemists pronounced, sadly.

"Dumb!—For heaven's sake!" objected a biologist. "Besides, even if it were true, when was that ever a disadvantage? As it is, she talks plenty—to no purpose."

"That's what I was meaning," the chemist explained patiently. "She's dumb along the wrong lines—the one way almost any good-looking girl isn't; and oughtn't to be," he added, for clarity.

Wives and concerned maidens allowed themselves, cautiously, to relax a little.

"Cold!" they told one another hopefully, not without undertones of self-satisfaction—yet not with unalloyed smugness, either, for a suspicion that someone may be quite indifferent to one's menfolk is not entirely welcome. However, the majority felt reassured by this provisional classification, though with a reservation caused mainly by her clothes; it was hard to believe that one could cast so much thought and care upon the waters with no expectation but to see it washed tracelessly away . . .

When Helen Daley, wife of Austin Daley, the biochemist who came nearest to being Darr's second-in-command, mentioned the problem, her husband took a divergent view.

"Whenever anyone new comes to this place there's always this spate of speculative natter. I don't understand why," he complained. "The young come bouncing along thinking they're wonderful, that the world begins with them, just as their parents did, and their grandparents did; they then get into just the same tangles, show the same intensities, and go on making the same mistakes as their parents and grandparents did. Thoroughly monotonous: they're all going to turn out to be one of four or five types, anyway; and only interesting if one is trying to have one's youth over again—which God forbid."

"I enjoyed being young," said his wife.

"You enjoy having been young—so do I," her husband corrected her. "But not again, thank you, not again."

"But I *did* enjoy it. Excitement, colors, lovely dresses, wonderful parties, moonlight rides, the thrill of a new affair..."

"Like the wonderful summers of one's childhood? Forgetting the disappointments, the hatred of rivals, the bitterness of losing, the wretchedness of being left out, the hurt of a careless word, the torments and anxieties, the tears on the pillow...? No, even the memory of youth's a stuff will not endure. The golden girls and boys lived in a golden age."

"It's no good pretending to me that you're an old cynic, Austin."

"My love, I am not a cynic, I confess. But neither am I a retrospective visionary. Therefore I am sorry for these young men and maidens who are going through the painful process of sloughing their illusions before emerging as a type, but I still think that for the observer it is a monotonous process."

"Well, to bring it round to where we were, what type do you think our latest recruit will turn out to be?"

"Young Diana? Early to say. She's what they call now a late-developer. At present she has a schoolgirl crush on our Francis."

"Oh, surely not..."

"There's no surely not about it. He may not be your model, but he's well designed for some others' father-figure, is Francis. I've observed it before. Doubtless I shall observe it again. He, of course, won't see it at all; he never does. All the same, she is an unusual young woman, and I'd take no bets on what course she'll follow when it wears off."

Whether Austin Daley was right or not, there was certainly no interesting development of Diana's personality during her first weeks at Darr. She simply continued to go her own way in not unamiable independence. Her acquaintanceship with male members of the staff either kept to a comradely note, or grew distant, and this unpoachful disposition gradually put her on good terms with a number of the young women, so that by degrees she began to scoop out a niche for herself as an oddity. The devotion of so much care to a decorative appearance came, with reservations, to be regarded as a quirk; a kind of artform, like flower arrangement, or water-color sketching, practiced by Diana apparently for her own entertainment, and its acceptance as such was helped by the discovery that she was willing to give really useful instruction in this hobby, upon request. An arrested form of amusement, it was felt—though not actually troublesome as long as it continued under arrest. Expensive, though. There was general conjecture that all her salary, if not more, must go on her clothes and décor.

"An odd child altogether," Caroline Saxover remarked. "She has the brains for one kind of life, and *some* of the tastes that go with quite another. Just at present she seems to be becalmed in a kind of doldrum between them, and not much interested in getting out of it. She'll probably come to life quite suddenly."

"Meaning that we shall suddenly find ourselves with another of these emotional *divertisements,* and lose another good worker?" Francis said gloomily. "I'm beginning to get reactionary. Wondering whether young women above a certain level of plainness should be allowed to squander the time of higher educationalists at all. It's become one of the expensive items in our economy of waste. Still, I suppose even a plainness test wouldn't guarantee anything. All the same, I do keep on hoping that some day we shall be able to get together a few girls whose individual purpose is greater than their herd instinct."

"Wouldn't you be meaning sex instinct, rather than herd?" Caroline suggested.

"Would I? I don't know. Is there any difference where young women are concerned?" Francis grumbled. "Anyway, let's hope this one resists it for more than a month or two."

Mrs. Brackley, confiding in her husband, took the opposite view.

"She seems quite contented with the place," she observed to her husband, after one of Diana's weekend visits home. "It's not nice to know that, though, of course, it's not likely she'll be there very long. Not a girl like Diana."

It was not a statement which seemed to call for comment, so Mr. Brackley made none.

"She seems to have a great admiration for this Dr. Saxover," his wife added.

"So have lots of people," Mr. Brackley told her. "He's got a considerable reputation among scientists. The people I asked about him were quite impressed when I told them Diana was working there. It apparently counts for something to get taken on at all."

"He's married, with two children. A boy of twelve, and a girl nearly ten," she remarked.

"Well, that's all right then. Or do you mean it isn't?" he said.

"Don't be ridiculous, Harold. A man nearly twice her age."

"All right," he agreed peaceably. "But what are we talking about?"

"Just that she seems to like it all right at present, but that from what she says it isn't the sort of place where an attractive girl like Diana ought to bury herself for long. There's her future to think of."

To which Mr. Brackley once more said nothing. He could never decide whether Diana's kindly determination to make common ground with her mother really deceived her, or whether his wife's notion that every daughter is a sort of production line puppet was simply unconquerable.

In the meantime Diana settled into Darr. Francis Saxover found her a good worker, and was relieved not to observe any sign of herd instinct that suggested imminent migration. Her relations with her colleagues continued for the most part to be amiable, though somewhat detached. On rare occasions she would let loose a bolt which made some of them blink, look at her twice, and wonder a little. But she used restraint, almost deliberately made little mark upon the community once she had repelled would-be boarders, and kept her own counsel equably enough to be taken for a decorative but otherwise unremarkable part of the scene.

"With us, but not of us," Austin Daley remarked of her at the end of the second month. "There's more in that girl than she is allowing to meet the eye. She has a way of smiling at the wrong things. Should be surprising, sooner or later."

3

On a morning after Diana had been some eight months at Darr the door of the room where she was working opened abruptly. She lifted her head from her microscope to perceive Francis Saxover standing in the doorway, with a saucer in his hand, and a pained expression on his face.

"Miss Brackley," he said, "I am told that it is a kindly concern of yours to see that Felicia is sustained during her nocturnal activities. If it really is necessary—which I doubt, since she doesn't seem to have touched your gift, but if it is—would you mind placing your saucer in a less traffic-prone situation in future. This is the third time I have almost fallen over my own feet in avoiding it."

"Oh, I'm so sorry, Dr. Saxover," Diana apologized. "I usually remember to take it away when I come up. She generally does drink it, you know. Perhaps the thunderstorm last night scared her."

She took the saucer of milk from his hand, and carried it across to the bench.

"I'll certainly see that—" In the act of putting the saucer down she broke off, and bent to look at it more closely.

During the thundery night the milk in it had "turned." At least, nearly all of it had turned, but there was a spot, a little under half-an-inch in diameter centered upon a dark speck, that looked different. It appeared not to have turned.

"That's funny," she said.

Francis glanced at the saucer, and then looked at it more carefully.

"What were you working on yesterday, just before you poured this out?" he asked her.

"That new batch of lichens. The Macdonald lot. I was on them nearly all day," she told him.

"H'm," said Francis.

He found a clean slide, fished out the speck, and put it on the slide.

"Can you identify?" he asked.

Diana took the slide to the microscope. Francis glanced at the little jumbles of gray-green "leaves" under various glass covers. They had a dreary look. Diana's inspection did not take long.

"It's from this lot," she said, indicating a pile of desiccated fragments variegated by yellow spots along the edges. "Provisionally," she explained, "I've called it *Lichenis Imperfectus Tertius Mongolensis Secundus Macdonaldi*."

"Have you indeed," remarked Francis.

"Well," she told him, defensively, "it isn't easy, you know. Nearly all lichens seem to be imperfecti anyway, and this happens to be the third one I tackled out of the second Macdonald batch."

"Well, we must remember that the name is provisional," Francis said.

"Antibiotic? Do you think?" Diana asked, glancing at the saucer again.

"It could be. Quite a number of lichens do have some antibiotic properties, so it isn't unlikely. It's a hundred to one against it being a *useful* antibiotic, of course. Still, it doesn't do to skip chances. I'll take a look at it, and let you know."

He picked up an empty jar and filled it with the lichen, leaving about half the heap still under its cover. Then he turned to go. But before he reached the door Diana's voice stopped him.

"Dr. Saxover, how is Mrs. Saxover today?" she asked.

He turned back, looking a different man, as if he had taken off a mask to reveal the wretchedness beneath. He shook his head slowly.

"The hospital says she's quite cheerful this morning. I hope it's true. It's all they *can* say. She doesn't know, you see. She still thinks the operation was successful. I suppose it is the best way—oh yes, it *is* the best way—but, oh God . . . !"

Then he turned to the door again, and was gone before Diana could say anything more.

The lichen went with him, and that was almost the last Diana officially heard of it for a long time.

Caroline Saxover died a few days later.

Francis seemed to go about in a trance. His widowed sister, Irene, arrived and did her best to take over that part of the domestic arrangements that Caroline had managed. Francis seemed scarcely to notice her. She tried to get him to go away for a time, but he would not. For a fortnight, or more, he roamed the place like the inversion of a ghost—his body present, but his spirit elsewhere. Then suddenly he was not to be seen at all. He shut himself up in his own laboratory. His sister sent meals up to him, but often they were not touched. He scarcely emerged for days, and often his bed was unused.

Austin Daley, who more or less forced his way in there, reported that he seemed to be working like a madman on half a dozen things at once, and predicted a breakdown. On the few occasions that he did appear at meals his manner was so distant and strained that the children were half afraid of him. Diana found Zephanie weeping miserably one afternoon. She did her best to comfort her, and took her along to her own lab and let her amuse herself with a microscope. The next day, a Saturday, she took the child for a twelve-mile walk to get her out of the place.

Meanwhile, the work in hand went on somehow, and Austin Daley did his best to manage what could be dealt with, and keep the place on its feet. Fortunately, he was aware of several projects that Francis had in mind, and was able to start them off. Occasionally he prevailed upon Francis to sign a few necessary papers, but he spent much time stalling off decisions that only Francis could, but would not, make. Darr began to show signs of silting up, and its personnel became restless.

Francis, however, did not have a breakdown. He was probably saved from it by getting pneumonia. He got it badly too, but when he slowly started to pick up strength again, it appeared to have broken the trauma, for it was almost as his normal self that he gradually revived.

But it was his normal self with a difference.

"Daddy's quieter than he used to be, and sort of gentler, too," Zephanie confided to Diana. "Sometimes it makes me want to cry."

"He was very, very fond of your mother. He must be feeling terribly lonely without her," said Diana.

"Yes," agreed Zephanie, "but he does talk about her now, and that's much better. He *likes* to talk about her, even if it does make him sad. But he spends an awful lot of time just sitting and thinking, and not looking sad at all. More like somebody working out sums."

"I expect that's what he is doing," Diana told her. "It takes a lot of working out of sums to keep Darr going, you know. And things did get a bit out of hand while he was ill. Probably he's just thinking about tidying everything up again, and it'll be all right once it's straight."

"I hope so. He looks as if they're such awfully difficult sums," said Zephanie.

What with one thing and another the question of the possible antibiotic qualities of *Lichenis Tertius Etcetera* dropped out of Diana's mind, and only recurred there after a few months. She felt sure that it must have been driven out of Francis's too, or she would have heard something. For one of Francis's scrupulosities was not to poach credit. Discoveries, and the patents and copyrights that covered them, became the property of Darr House Developments, but credit belonged to individuals, or to teams. Human nature being what it is, it cannot be said that everyone was always entirely satisfied with his degree of credit—it is, for instance, a matter of some nicety to apportion fairly between the man who had the idea itself, and the man who supplied the germ of it—but it was generally conceded, and appreciated, that Francis took pains to be just, and to see to it that no suggestion was either incorrectly ascribed, or lost in anonymity—nor allowed to sink without trace. Had things been normal, therefore, Diana was quite sure that she would have heard something of *Lichenis Tertius,* positive, negative, or interim. As conditions were, she assumed, when she did recollect the matter several months later, that the jar of lichen must have been put aside somewhere about the time of Caroline Saxover's death, and its contents left to molder away. With Francis's recovery, however, it recurred to her that a note of some kind should be entered regarding the nature of the properties observed in *Tertius,* if only for the record. She decided that at some convenient moment she would remind him, and then kept on forgetting to do so when discussion on other matters drove it out of her mind. In the end, it was during one of the monthly soirées that Caroline had instituted to help Darr's sense of community that the recollection and the opportunity came together, prompted, possibly, by the arrival of another bale of botanical oddments from the far-wandering Mr. Macdonald.

During refreshments, Francis, now almost his former self

again, was following his usual practice of chatting with one and another of his staff. Encountering Diana, he thanked her for the kindnesses she had shown to his daughter.

"It's made a great difference to her. Somebody to take an interest in her and rouse her own interests was just what she needed most in the circumstances, poor child," he told her. "It's meant a lot to her, I know, and I am immensely grateful to you."

"Oh, but I enjoy it," Diana told him. "We get on well together. She makes me feel like a not too elder sister, and I try to make her feel like a not too young one. I always regretted I didn't have a sister of my own, so perhaps I'm compensating. At any rate Zephanie's much too good company for me ever to have thought it a chore."

"I'm glad. She's full of your praises. But you mustn't let her impose upon you."

"I won't," Diana assured him. "Not that it's like to be necessary. She's a very perceptive child, you know."

And then, a few minutes later, when he had been about to continue his round, the question had jumped into her mind.

"Oh, by the way, Dr. Saxover, I've been meaning to ask you before, do you remember that Macdonald lichen—the *Tertius* one, back in June or July?—Did it turn out to be interesting?"

She asked the question almost casually, half-expecting him to say he'd forgotten about it. To her surprise, for a brief but unmistakable moment, he looked startled. He covered up quickly, but the look had been there, and, too, he hesitated for a moment before he replied. Then he said:

"Oh, dear! How reprehensible of me. I ought to have let you know long ago. No, I'm afraid I was mistaken there. It turned out not to be an antibiotic after all."

A few moments later he had moved on to speak to someone else.

At the time Diana had only half-consciously noted that there was something a little amiss with that reply. It was later that she began to appreciate that it was a silly thing for Francis to have said. And even then she was half-inclined to attribute it to the strain and illness he had suffered. But it went on niggling at the back of her mind. If he had told her that he had forgotten all about it, been too busy with other things to deal with it, or that its action was too widely toxic for it to be worth following up, or given one of half a dozen other reasons, she would quite likely have been satisfied. But for some reason the question had caught him off-balance, and brought an ill-considered reply—a reply, which, when you thought about it, dodged a direct answer. Why should he want to dodge it?

Somehow she found herself recognizing "turned out not to be an antibiotic" not only for a slip, but for a particular kind of slip. The sort of slip that would be made by a man taken by surprise who was too naturally truthful to be swift with a lie . . .

On closer consideration, then, the implication of the unguarded reply was scarcely to be escaped: the *Tertius* lichen certainly had a property which *looked* antibiotic; but if it had turned out *not* to be antibiotic, then what had it turned out to be . . . ?

And why should Francis wish to conceal it . . . ?

Why the question went on worrying away in the second layer of her thoughts to the extent it did, Diana never quite understood. Later, she tentatively ascribed it to incongruity: the apparently petty evasiveness which was in such contrast with her opinion of Francis, with his reputation, and with his usual manner. All she knew at the time was that it did go on niggling.

Then came another factor. The stores department sent a note asking her to turn in her materials for quantity checking. Obediently, she began to list them, and then, when she reached *Lichenis Tertius,* etc., in her list, two observations suddenly linked themselves together: one was that only a few days before she had mentioned *Tertius* to Francis at the soirée; the other, that the stores department's request came, as a matter of routine, on a Monday, not on a Friday, and that the regular quarterly checking was due to take place in two weeks' time, anyway.

Diana sat looking at the item for several minutes. She was attempting to resist an urge—not an ordinary temptation for it had none of the flavor of temptation, nor any prospect of gain, but something more like curiosity raised to a compulsion. And in the end it won.

"I did," she said later on, "I did a thing I despised, that I had thought myself incapable of. I deliberately falsified my returns. And what was so queer was that I felt no guilt or shame as I did it, but rather as if it were a distasteful necessity."

And so the bundle of *Lichenis Tertius* that had been sorted out of the latest Macdonald parcel never appeared on the register at all.

—

In the early stages of her investigation of the lichen, Diana had one advantage over Francis; she was not working under the impression that she was dealing with an antibiotic. She knew only that she was seeking something which had one property that looked antibiotic, but was not. She decided also from Francis's manner that it was something unusual, possibly dangerous; but that was of little help except insofar as it prepared her to let her mind work on broad lines over her findings. In spite of this, however, she all but rejected the very thing she was looking for, as too improbable. Then, on the very verge of dismissing it she hesitated. However improbable, it was not a confirmed impossibility. For good order, if for no other reason, it deserved a further test . . . and then another . . . and another . . .

Years later she said:

"It wasn't intuition, and it wasn't common sense. It began with a logical inference, was all but wrecked by prejudice, and then saved by system. I could have easily missed it and gone on the wrong lines for months, so I suppose there was an element of luck, too. Even when I'd checked and re-checked, I didn't really believe it—at least I was in a kind of schizoid state; my professional self had proved it and failed to disprove it, so it had to believe it; but my off-duty self couldn't genuinely accept it any more intimately than one accepts the proposition that the world is round. I suppose that is what made me so astonishingly dumb about it. I just did not begin to see the implications that were staring me in the face; not for weeks, months afterward. It was simply an interesting scientific discovery which I intended to develop to a useful stage, so I concentrated on the real job of isolating the active agent, and gave scarcely a thought to the consequences. A bit like people who breed on religious principles, when you come to think of it."

The work became a challenge to Diana. It took almost all her spare time, and she frequently worked late into the evenings. Her weekend visits home became irregular, and she was restless when she was there. Zephanie, who had been sent off to boarding school, was disappointed to see little of her during the holidays.

"You're *always* working," she complained. "You look tired, too."

"It won't be much longer now, I think," Diana told her. "Unless something very unexpected crops up I ought to be through with it in a month or two."

"What is it all about?" Zephanie wanted to know. But Diana had shaken her head.

"Too complicated," she said. "I just couldn't explain it to anyone who hasn't done a lot of chemistry."

Her experiments were conducted mostly upon mice, and by the late autumn, more than a year after Caroline Saxover's death, she was beginning to have real confidence in her results. In the meantime, she had discovered the group of animals that Francis had been using for his tests, and it was encouraging to be able to keep an eye on them, too. By that time the true work was over. The results were proved beyond any doubt. What remained was steady experimentation which would provide enough data to give close, reliable control of the process—routine work which took comparatively little time, and allowed her to relax—And it was not until she did begin to relax that she really started to think about what she had found . . .

In the early stages of the work she had occasionally speculated on Francis's attitude, and wondered what he intended to do with his findings. Now she started to give the matter her full attention. Uneasily she realized that his work must have been fully six months ahead of hers. He must have been perfectly sure of his findings, and of the practicability of their application, right back in the summer, yet there had not been a whisper of them. That in itself was odd. Francis trusted his staff. He maintained that secrecy, unless it was absolutely necessary, lowered efficiency, and deteriorated the sense of corporate endeavor. His staff responded, and there had seldom been any premature leakages from Darr. On the other hand, it meant that inside Darr there was seldom any project in hand that you could not pick up at least a few hints about if you tried. But of this there had been nothing; not the least zephyr. As far as she could tell he had done all the work on it himself, and kept the results entirely to himself. It might be that he had negotiations for its large-scale production by manufacturers in hand, but somehow she thought not—even at that stage she was half aware that it was too big a matter to be handled in the usual way. So she decided that he would probably read a paper on it before one of the Societies. In that case, she would of course have to hand over her own work at once—but if he did so intend, she did not altogether understand the need for so efficient a cloak of secrecy among his own staff at a stage when his data must be quite complete. . . .

So Diana decided to wait and see. . . .

She felt troubled, too, by her ethical position which looked more than a little moot. Not the legal position; there, she was fairly and squarely in the wrong. Under the usual clause in her contract any discovery made by her while in the employ of Darr House Developments Ltd became the property of Darr House. Legally, she was aware, she should have handed the whole thing over to Francis straight away. But ethically was different.... Well, look at it. If she had not dropped the lichen in the milk there'd have been no discovery. If Francis had not brought in the saucer the effect might never have been noticed. If she had not noticed it, he would have missed it. She had not stolen Francis's work in any way. Really, you could say, she had been prompted by curiosity into investigating a phenomenon which she had observed for herself. She had worked hard on it, and arrived under her own steam. It struck her as pretty grim to have to let it all go—unless it were really necessary. So she would temporize and see what move Francis intended to make.

Waiting gave more time for thinking; and thinking gave more grounds for uneasiness. She found herself able to stand back a little so that the trees merged into a wood, and a pretty ominous-looking wood it came to seem. Implications that she had never thought of before started to crawl out of it in all directions. Gradually she perceived that Francis must have perceived them, too, and she began to have some understanding of the considerations that might be holding him back.

And, little by little, as she went on waiting, the wider view of the whole position built itself up like a jigsaw puzzle in her mind until the vista alarmed her. Only then did she begin to appreciate that this was not just another interesting discovery, but something cardinal: that they were holding one of the most valuable, and explosive, secrets in the world. And only after that was she gradually forced to the realization that Francis, Francis Saxover of all people, did not know what to do with it....

Years later she said: "I think now that I made a mistake in doing nothing then—in just going on waiting. Once I began to understand a little about the consequences, I should have gone to him, and told him what I'd done. At the very least, it would have given him someone to talk to about it—and that might have helped him to decide how to deal with it. But he was a famous man. He was my boss. I was nervous because my position was—well, equivocal, to put it kindly. Worst of all, I was young enough to be badly shocked."

That, perhaps, was the real barrier. Even back in her schooldays Diana had accepted as an article of faith the proposition that knowledge was no less a gift of God than life itself; from which it followed that the suppression of knowledge was a sin against the light. She would no longer have used such terms to express herself, but the sense of them held firm. The seeker after knowledge did not seek for himself; he was under a special Commandment: to deliver to all men whatever he might be privileged to learn.

The thought that one of the leaders in her calling could seem to be breaking that Commandment appalled her; that it should be Francis Saxover, whom she venerated and had regarded as the epitome of professional integrity hurt her so deeply that she was utterly bewildered....

"I was young for my age—still hard and perfectionist. Francis had been an ideal, and he wasn't running true to the type I had cast him for. It's all very self-centered really. I couldn't forgive him for clay-feet; it seemed as if he had let *me* down. I was in a frightful muddle, and all skewered through with my own rigid ideas. It was hell. One of those growing shocks, the worst I ever had, when it seems as if something had gone out, and the world can never be the same again—and, of course, it never is...."

The consequence of the shock was a hardening of her resolution. She would not even contemplate letting Francis know anything about her own work on the lichen. He could commit the crime of suppressing knowledge and have it on his conscience, but she was not going to be an accessory. She would wait just a little longer, in the hope that he would change his mind, but if he still showed no signs of publishing, or applying, the discovery, she would go ahead herself, and see that it was given to the world. . . .

So then Diana began to consider the effects more fully, which turned out to mean, largely, that she was studying obstacles. The closer the attention she gave the matter, the more dismayed she became by the number and variety of interests that were *not* going to welcome the lichen derivative. It turned out to be far from the straightforward choice, to speak, or not to speak, that it had appeared. She began to have a much clearer understanding of the dilemma that Francis must have reached months before. But she would not let it be a sympathetic understanding; instead, it was a challenge: if he could not solve it, she would. . . .

She went on pondering the problem through the winter, but when the spring came, she was no nearer a solution.

On her twenty-fifth birthday she came into her inheritance from her grandfather's estate, and was astonished to find herself well off. She celebrated by buying some clothes from famous houses that she had never hoped to enter, and a small car. To her mother's amazement she did not decide to leave Darr at once.

"But why should I, Mummy? What should I do with myself? I like the country there, and the work's interesting and useful," she said.

"But now that you have an independent income—" her mother protested.

"I know, darling. A sensible girl would go out and buy herself a husband."

"I certainly wouldn't put it like that, dear. But, after all, a woman ought to be married; she's happier that way. You're twenty-five now, you know. If you don't think seriously about raising a family now—well, time doesn't stand still. Thirty's on you before you know it, then forty. Life isn't very long. You see that plainly when you begin to look at it from the other end. Not time to do very much."

"I'm not at all sure that I do want to raise a family," Diana told her. "There are so many families already."

Mrs. Brackley looked shocked.

"But every woman wants a family, at heart," she said. "It's only natural."

"Habitual," corrected Diana. "God knows what would happen to civilization if we did things just because they were natural."

Mrs. Brackley frowned.

"I don't understand you, Diana. Don't you *want* a house of your own, and a family?"

"Not furiously, Mummy, or I expect I'd have done something about it long before this. Perhaps I'll try it, though, later on. I might like it. I've plenty of time yet."

"Not so long as you think. A woman is always up against time, and it doesn't do to forget it."

"I'm sure you're right, darling. But being too conscious of it can produce some pretty ghastly results as well, don't you think? Don't you worry about me, Mummy. I know what I'm doing."

So, for the time being, Diana stayed at Darr.

Zephanie, coming home for the Easter holidays, complained that she was preoccupied.

"You don't look tired like you did when you were working so hard," she conceded, "but you do *think* such a dreadful lot."

"Well, you have to think in my job. That's what it is, mostly," retorted Diana.

"But not *all* the time."

"Perhaps it's not entirely me. Now, *you* don't think as much as you did before you went to that school. If you just go on taking what they tell you without thinking about it, you'll turn into advertisers' meat, and end up as a housewife."

"But most people do—become housewives, I mean," Zephanie said.

"I know they do—housewife, hausfrau, house-woman, housekeeper, house-minder. Is that what you want? It's a diddle word, darling. Tell a woman: 'woman's place is in the home,' or 'get thee to thy kitchen' and she doesn't like it; but call it 'being a good housewife,' which means exactly the same thing, and she'll drudge along, glowing with pride.

"My great-aunt fought, and went to prison several times, for women's rights; and what did she achieve? A change of technique from coercion to diddle, and a generation of granddaughters who don't even know they're being diddled—and probably wouldn't care more if they did. Our deadliest susceptibility is conformity, and our deadliest virtue is putting up with things as they are. So watch for the diddles, darling. You can't be too careful about them in a world where the symbol of the joy of living can be a baked bean."

Zephanie received the advice in silence, but was not to be entirely diverted by it. She asked:

"You're not unhappy, are you, Diana? I mean, it isn't that sort of thinking you keep on doing is it?"

"Good gracious, no, darling. It's just problems."

"More like geometry kind of problems?"

"Well, yes, I suppose so—sort of human geometry. I'm sorry they oppress you. I'll try to forget them for a bit. Let's take the car out somewhere, shall we?"

But the problems continued to be problems. And Diana's growing conviction that Francis had given up, and decided to shelve the whole matter only made her the more determined to find a solution.

The summer came on. In June she went with a Cambridge friend for a holiday in Italy. Friend proved highly susceptible to Latin charm, even to the extent of getting—rather temporarily, as it turned out—engaged. Diana, too, enjoyed herself, but returned (alone) with little regret, and a feeling that too much of that sort of thing must pretty soon cloy.

She had been back at Darr a fortnight when Zephanie's school broke up once more, and she came home for a part of the summer holidays.

One evening they strolled out into the big meadow just shorn of its second crop, and sat leaning comfortably against a haycock. Diana inquired how Zephanie had got on this term.

Not so badly, Zephanie thought modestly, at least, not so badly with work, and not so badly with tennis, but she didn't think much of cricket. Diana agreed about cricket.

"Very dull," she said. "It's a vestige of emancipation. Freedom for girls meant having to do what boys did, however boring."

Zephanie went on to give an account of her term, mingled with her opinions of school life. At the end, Diana nodded.

"Well, at least they don't seem to be training *you* exclusively for housewifery," she said, with mild approval.

Zephanie considered the implications of that a bit.

"Aren't you going to get married, Diana?"

"Oh, I daresay I shall—one day," Diana conceded.

"But if you don't, what'll you do? Will you be like your great-aunt, and fight for women's rights?"

"You've got it a bit muddled, darling. My great-aunt, and other people's great-aunts, won all the rights that women need ages ago. All that's been lacking since then is the social courage to use them. My great-aunt and the rest thought that by technically defeating male privilege they'd scored a great victory. What they didn't realize is that the greatest enemies of women aren't men at all, they are women: silly women, lazy women, and smug women. Smug women are the worst; their profession is being women, and they just hate any women who make any other kind of profession a success. It sets up an inferiority-superiority thing in them."

Zephanie regarded her thoughtfully.

"I don't think you like women very much, Diana," she decided.

"Too sweeping, darling. What I don't like about us is our readiness to be conditioned—the easy way we can be made to be *willing* to be nothing better than squaws and second-class citizens, and taught to go through life as appendages instead of as people in our own right."

Zephanie considered again. She said:

"I told Miss Roberts—she takes us for history—what you said about the change from forcing women to do things to simply diddling them into them."

"Oh, did you? And what did she say?"

"She agreed, really. But she said, well, this is the kind of world we have to live in. There is so very much that's wrong with it, but then life is so short that the best anyone can do is to come to terms with it while doing her best to preserve her own standards. She said it would be different if we had more time to spare, but now there isn't enough margin to make people do things about it. By the time your children have grown up you're beginning to get old, so it isn't worth trying to do much, and then in another twenty-five years it will be the same for them, and— Why, Diana, what on earth's the matter ... ?"

But Diana did not reply. She sat staring straight before her, gray eyes wide open, as if mesmerized.

"Diana—aren't you well?" Zephanie pulled at her sleeve.

Diana turned her head slowly, not really seeing her.

"That's *it!*" she said. "My God—that's it! There it was, staring me in the face all the time, and I never saw it. ..."

She put her hand to her forehead and leaned back against the hay. Zephanie bent over her anxiously.

"Diana, what's wrong? Can I get something?"

"There's nothing wrong, Zephanie darling. Nothing at all. It's just that I've found out what I'm going to do."

"What do you mean?" Zephanie asked, bewildered.

"I've found my career. . . ." Diana told her, in an odd voice. Then she began to laugh. She leaned back against the haycock, and went on laughing, and half-crying, too, in such a queer way that Zephanie was alarmed. . . .

The next day Diana sought an interview with Francis, and explained that she would like to leave at the end of August.

Francis sighed. He glanced at her left hand, and then looked puzzled.

"Oh," he exclaimed, "not the routine reason?"

She had seen his glance.

"No," she said.

"You ought to have borrowed one," he told her. "This leaves me free to argue."

"I don't want to argue," Diana told him.

"But you must. I've been known to argue with valuable members of my staff even when Hymen is standing in the wings. When he's not, I always argue. Now, what is it? What have we done—or are we not doing?"

The interview, which Diana had hoped would be briefly formal, went on for some time. She explained that she had come into some money, and intended to take a trip round the world. He did not disapprove of that. In fact: "Good idea," he said, "give you a chance to see for yourself how some of our tropical stuff really does in the field. Don't hurry it. Take a year off. Consider it a sort of Sabbatical."

"No," Diana said firmly. "That's not what I mean."

"You don't want to come back here? I wish you would. We shall miss you, you know. I don't mean just professionally."

"Oh, that's not it at all," she told him, wretchedly. "I—I—" she dried up, and remained staring at him.

"If someone offered you a better job . . . ?"

"Oh, no—no. I'm just giving up."

"You mean, getting out of research altogether?"

She nodded.

"But that's preposterous, Diana. With a talent like yours, why—" He went on at some length, and then broke off, looking back at the gray eyes, suddenly aware that she had heard nothing of what he had said. "It isn't like you at all. There must be a good reason," he told her.

Diana stood uncertain, hesitating as if she were on a perilous brink.

"I—" she began again, and then stopped as if she were choking.

She went on facing him across the desk. He saw that she was trembling. Before he could move to help her, an astonishing conflict of emotions broke through her usually calm expression, as if a fierce, alarming, internal struggle were taking place.

He got up to move round the desk to her, and she seemed to get back partial control. She said, almost gasping:

"No—no! You must let me go, Francis. You must let me go."

And she fled from the room before he could reach her.

Part TWO

4

"I'm glad you were both able to get away," Francis told his children.

"*I* ought not to be here, but you did make it sound pretty urgent," Paul said.

"It is important certainly, but just how urgent still seems to be in doubt. I hoped to know myself by now, but the fourth member of our quartet has been delayed. I doubt whether you'll remember her. She left Darr nearly fourteen years ago now—Diana Brackley."

"I think I do," Paul told him. "Tall, rather distinguished-looking, wasn't she?"

"I certainly do, very well," Zephanie put in. "I had a pash for Diana. I used to think she was the most beautiful, and next to you, Daddy, the cleverest person in the world. I cried like anything when she went away."

"It's a long time ago. I don't see how she can have anything really urgent to tell us. What's it about?" asked Paul.

"That needs quite a little preliminary explanation," Francis told him. "In fact, perhaps it's as well that she's been delayed. It will give me a chance to clear some of the ground first."

He gazed critically at his son and daughter. Paul, twenty-seven now, and an engineer, still looked boyish in spite of the beard with which he attempted to give himself more authority.

Zephanie had grown up to be much prettier than he had expected. She had her mother's curling golden hair, his own structure of face, femininely softened, and dark hazel eyes that she got from neither of them. As she sat now in his study, in a cotton summer dress, her hair not fully tamed after her drive to Darr, she looked more like a girl about to leave school than a member of a university engaged upon a post-graduate course.

"You are almost certainly going to think that this is something I should have told you before. Perhaps that is so, but there seemed to me to be good reasons against it. I hope you will see that, when you have had time to consider."

"Oh dear. This sounds terribly ominous, Daddy. Are we foundlings, or something?" Zephanie asked.

"No. You're certainly not. But it is rather a long story, and to make it clear I'd better start at the beginning, and try to condense it. It began in the July of the year your mother died. . . ."

He gave them an account of the finding of the lichen speck in the saucer of milk, and went on:

"I took the jar of lichen up to my own lab to be looked at later. Soon after that your mother died. I went rather to pieces over it, I think—it's not at all clear now, but I remember waking up one morning and knowing quite suddenly that if I didn't get down to some work and lose myself in it I should crack up altogether. So I went off to the lab and worked. There were half a dozen things there waiting for me, and I worked on them pretty much night and day to keep my mind occupied. One of the things I looked into was that lichen that Diana had spotted.

"Lichens are queer things. They're not single organisms, you know. They are actually two life forms living in symbiosis—fungi and algae, interdependent. For a long time there didn't seem to be any use for them except that one kind is the reindeer's food, and others produce dyes. Then comparatively recently some of them had been found to have antibiotic properties of which usnic acid is the most common agent, but there was, and still is, a great deal of work to be done on them.

"Naturally, I thought, as anyone would, that an antibiotic was what I was looking for. And to some extent that lichen seemed to have such a property, but—oh, well, we can go into the details some other time—the point is that after a while I had to recognize that it was *not* an antibiotic, and was gradually forced to admit that it was something quite different. Something there was no name for. So I had to invent one. I called it an antigerone."

Paul looked puzzled. Zephanie said, forthrightly:

"Meaning what, Daddy?"

"Anti—against; gerone—age, or, more literally, an old man. Nobody seems to mind mixing Latin and Greek roots nowadays, so—antigerone. One could have been more accurate, but it will do.

"The active concentrate derived from the lichen I call simply 'lichenin.' The actual physico-chemical details of the actions and effects upon the living organism are extremely complex and require a great deal of study, but the total effect is quite straightforward in its results: it simply retards the normal rate of metabolism throughout the organism."

His son and daughter were silent while the implication sank. It was Zephanie who spoke first.

"Daddy—Daddy, you don't mean you've found—Oh, no, it can't be *that*!"

"It is, darling. That's what it is," he told her.

Zephanie sat quite still staring at him, unable to express anything of what she was feeling.

"*You*, Daddy, *you*—!" she said, still barely credulous.

Francis smiled.

"Even I, my dear—though you mustn't give me too much credit for it. Someone was bound to come across it quite soon. It just happened to be me."

"Just happened—my God!" said Zephanie. "Like it *just happened* to be Fleming with penicillin. Gosh, Daddy. I—I feel quite queer..."

She got up and crossed the floor a little uncertainly to the window. There she stood with her forehead pressed to the cool glass, looking out across the park.

Paul said, in a bewildered way:

"I'm sorry, Dad, but I'm afraid I don't fully get this. It seems to have knocked Zeph endways, so it must be quite something, but I'm only a plain civil engineer, remember."

"It isn't very difficult to understand—it's believing it that comes harder at first," Francis began to explain. "Now the processes of cell division and growth—"

Zephanie, at the window, suddenly stiffened. Abruptly she swung round to face the room. Her gaze fastened on her father's profile, studying him intently, then it moved to a large framed photograph of him standing beside Caroline, taken only a few months before her death, then back again to his face. Her eyes widened. With a curious, half-awake motion, she crossed to a wall mirror, and stood looking into it.

Francis broke off his disquisition to Paul in mid-sentence, and turned his head to watch her. Both he and she were perfectly still for some seconds. Zephanie's eyes became less wide. She shifted their focus, and spoke through the mirror without turning her head.

"How long?" she said.

Francis did not reply. He might not have heard her. His gaze left her and traveled across the wall to the portrait of his wife.

Zephanie caught her breath suddenly, and turned round, almost fiercely. The tension in her whole body hardened her voice.

"I asked you *how long*," she said. "How long am I going to live?"

Francis looked back. Their eyes held for a long moment, then his dropped. He studied his hands intently for a few seconds, then he looked up again. With a curious kind of pedantry flattening any emotion out of his voice, he replied:

"I estimate your expectation of life, my dear, at approximately two hundred and twenty years."

—

In the pause that followed there was a knock at the door. Miss Birchett, Francis's secretary, put her head in.

"Miss Brackley on the line from London, sir. She says it's important."

Francis nodded, and followed her out of the room, leaving his children staring after him.

"Did he really mean that?" Paul exclaimed.

"Oh, Paul! Can you imagine Daddy saying a thing like that if he didn't mean it?"

"No, I suppose not. Me, too?" he added in a bewildered way.

"Of course. Only it'll be a bit less for you," Zephanie told him.

She walked over to one of the armchairs, and dropped down into it.

"I don't see how you got on to it so fast," Paul said, with a touch of suspicion.

"Nor do I quite. It was like one of those puzzle things. He gave it a twist the right way, and it all slipped together quite suddenly."

"What slipped together?"

"Oh, things. Lots of little things."

"But, I don't get it. All he said was—"

He broke off as the door opened and Francis returned.

"Diana won't be coming down after all," Francis said. "The emergency is over, she says."

"What emergency?" Zephanie asked.

"I'm not altogether clear about that yet—except that she thought there might be publicity, and that she ought to warn me. That decided me that it was time you were told."

"But I don't understand. Where does Diana come into it? Is she acting as your agent, or something?" Zephanie wanted to know.

Francis shook his head.

"She is not my agent. Until a couple of days ago I'd no idea that anybody but me knew anything about it. However, she made it quite clear that she does, and has done for some time."

Paul frowned.

"I still don't— Do you mean she's stolen your work?"

"No," Francis told him. "I don't think that. She says she worked it out for herself, and can show me her notes to prove it. I'm willing to believe that. Whether, even as her own work, it is her rightful property or not, is a different matter."

"But what is the emergency about?" Zephanie asked.

"As I understand it, she has been using the lichenin. Something went wrong, and now she is being sued for damages. She's afraid that unless she can keep it out of court the whole thing may be shown in the evidence."

"And she can't, or doesn't want to, pay, so she'd like to borrow from you to keep it from coming to court?" Paul suggested.

"I wish you wouldn't keep on jumping to conclusions, Paul. You don't remember Diana, I do. It's some firm she's in that is being sued. They can pay, all right, she says, but they are caught in a cleft. The damages claimed are so high as to amount to blackmail. If they pay, it will encourage other people to try outrageous claims; if they don't, there'll be publicity. It's a very awkward situation."

"I don't see—" Zephanie began. Then she stopped. Her eyes widened. "Oh—you mean she's been giving this stuff—"

"Lichenin, Zephanie."

"Lichenin. She's been giving it to people without their knowing?"

"But of course she must have been. Do you think, if they *did* know, that the news wouldn't have been all round the world in about five minutes? Why do you think I was so careful that I've not even told you two about it until now? . . . In order to use it at all with safety I had to resort to a subterfuge; so, obviously, must she."

"Our immunization!" Paul exclaimed suddenly. "*That's* what it was."

He recalled a day soon after his seventeenth birthday when Francis had told him at some length about the resistance that certain bacteria had developed to the usual antibiotics, and had urged him to take advantage of a new immunizing agent that would not be generally available for a couple of years yet. There had been no reason why Paul should not agree, so they had gone up to the lab. There his father had made an incision in his arm, inserted a pellet shaped like a miniature whetstone, then closed the wound with a couple of stitches, and put a bandage on it.

"That'll last you a year," Francis had said, and ever since then it had become an annual event somewhere about the date of his birthday. Later on, when Zephanie was sixteen, he had done the same for her.

"Exactly. The immunization," Francis agreed.

They both sat staring at him for several seconds. Then Zephanie frowned.

"That's all very well, Daddy. We're us, and you're you, so it wasn't very difficult really. But it would be quite different for Diana. How on earth could she—?"

She broke off, struck by a sudden memory of Diana leaning back against a haycock and laughing so hysterically. What was it she had said? ". . . I've found out what I'm going to do. . . ."

"What is this firm of Diana's?" she asked.

Francis looked uncertain.

"Something odd," he said. "Egyptian—ridiculous sort of name—not Cleopatra."

"No—not *Nefertiti?*" suggested Zephanie.

"Yes, that's it. Nefertiti Ltd."

"Good heavens! And Diana is— No wonder she laughed," Zephanie exclaimed.

"A firm called Nefertiti sounds more preposterous than laughable to me," her father said. "What does it do?"

"Oh, dear, Daddy. Really! Where *do* you live? It just happens to be one of *the*—well, *the* beauty place in London. Terribly expensive and exclusive."

The implication did not reach Francis at once, but as it sank in a series of emotions began to conflict in his expression. He stared back at his daughter, bereft of speech. Then his eyes unfocused. He leaned suddenly forward, put his face in his hands, and began to laugh with a queer jerky sobbing.

Zephanie and Paul looked at one another for a startled moment. Paul hesitated. Then he went across to Francis, and put his hands on his shoulders. Francis seemed not to notice. Paul took a firmer hold, and gave a jerk.

"Father!" he said. "Stop it!"

Zephanie crossed to the cupboard and poured some brandy into a glass, with a shaky hand. She took it back. Francis was sitting up now, tears on his cheeks and a half-vacant expression in his eyes. He took the glass and drank half the contents at a gulp. Gradually his eyes lost their empty look.

"Sorry," he said. "But it is funny, isn't it? All these years. All these years a secret. Greatest discovery in centuries. Too big a secret. Say nothing to anybody. Too dangerous. And now *this*! A beauty treatment. . . . It *is* funny, isn't it? Don't you think it's funny?" He started to laugh again.

Zephanie put her arm round him, and held him to her.

"Sh!—Daddy. Lie back now, and try to relax. That's it, darling. Take another drink now. You'll feel better."

He leaned back in the corner of the couch, looking up into

her face. He dropped the empty glass onto the floor and reached for her free hand. He raised it and looked at it for a moment. He kissed it, and then lifted his eyes to his wife's portrait. "Oh, God!" he said, and wept.

—

After an hour and a half, and a good luncheon, Francis, quite restored, led them back to his study to continue his disquisition.

"As I told you," he said, "I take little credit for finding lichenin—it started from an accident, and Diana appears to have taken advantage of the same accident. The difficult part began when I realized what it was that I had found.

"There are quite half-a-dozen major discoveries only just below the horizon at this moment: and nobody is making the least attempt to prepare for any of them. An antigerone of some kind, possibly of several kinds, was virtually certain to show up before long, but I'd never heard of anyone who had given any serious thought to the problems it would raise. I had not the least idea how to deal with it myself, and the more I thought about it, the more alarmed I felt, because I began to appreciate that this thing is in the megaton range. It isn't as spectacular as the nuclear boys' fireworks, but it's more important—in its way it is more disruptive, but it is potentially a great deal more beneficial. . . .

"But just imagine the result of a public announcement . . . simply the superficial result of knowing that the means to extend one's term of life exists. The thing would be off like a prairie fire. Think of the newspapers fawning on it. One of the great wish-dreams of mankind come true at last. Think of twenty million copies of the *Reader's Compact* telling everyone in half-a-dozen languages: 'You, Too, Can Be Methuselah!' The contriving, the intriguing, the bribery—perhaps fighting, even—that would come of people trying to get in first to grab even a few extra years, and the chaos that would follow in a world which is already overpopulated, with a birthrate far too high. The whole prospect was—and is—quite appalling. Three or four centuries ago perhaps we could have absorbed the impact, and controlled it, but now, in the modern world . . . Well, it gave me nightmares. . . . It still does, sometimes. . . .

"But that wasn't the worst of it, by any means. Discovering it in the wrong century is bad enough, but I had done worse than that: I had discovered the wrong antigerone.

"I'm convinced that, since there is one, there must be others. They may be less efficient, or more efficient, but others there *must* be. The basic trouble with lichenin is that it is derived from a particular species of lichen that was sent to us by a roving botanist called Macdonald, and it exists in colonies which, as far as he knows, are restricted to a few square miles of territory. In other words there's precious little of it. What there is has to be conserved, and mustn't be cropped too heavily. According to my information it would yield enough to keep up the treatment for, say, three or four thousand people, but not many more.

"So one can see what would happen—or at least one can form some idea. You announce the discovery—and then qualify it by saying that only these three or four thousand can be treated. Well, my God, it's a matter of life and death—Who are going to be the lucky ones that are allowed to live longer? And why? Worse still, the value of the lichen would at once become astronomical. The stampede for it would be like a gold-rush—only swifter. In a week or two, perhaps even a few days, it would all be gone, wiped out. And that would be the end of lichenin. Finish!

"To get anything like the quantities of the derivative that would be needed, you'd have to cultivate the lichen over thousands of square miles, and it could not be done. Apart from acquiring the vast acreage of land that was suitable, you'd never be able to raise it because you'd never be able to guard it efficiently—the value would be too high.

"For nearly fifteen years now I've seen only one way out, and that is to find a method of synthesizing it—and that, I have so far failed to do. . . .

"The other possibility was that if one waited long enough somebody would almost certainly come up with another kind of antigerone, perhaps one derived from a plentiful source. But that was, and still is, one of those things that could happen tomorrow, or might take quite a long time. . . .

"Meanwhile, what was I to do? I badly needed someone to confide in. I wanted assistants to help me work on the synthesis. But the trouble was, who? How do you select people who are proof against temptation—temptation that could run into millions—for just a few key sentences? And even if you could, there's the other leakage problem—just a careless word or two, perhaps a mere hint that we were onto something of the kind would be enough to start some people speculating and investigating, and then, before long they'd be after it—then, as I said, poof—no more lichen . . . !

"I simply could not think of anyone I could bring myself to trust entirely. Probably in a situation like that one becomes somewhat obsessed. But, you see, get the most reliable fellow you know, then on *one* occasion he drops just *one* critical clue, and the damage is done . . . It came down to the fact that there was only one person I could have full control over, and that was myself. As long as I took all the care I could think of, and told no one at all, then it *couldn't* leak—that that was the only way I could be *sure* that it couldn't leak . . .

"But, on the other hand, if no one is to benefit from a discovery, it might as well not be made. I was entirely satisfied with my results on lab animals. The next stage was to try it on myself. I did that, and found the results just as satisfactory. Then came the question of you two.

"If anyone was entitled to the benefit of your father's discovery, surely it was you. But there, again, was the security problem. You were young. Keeping the secret would have been a great strain on you. And still there was the chance of a slip—and a small slip by either of you, coupled with the Saxover name, would be quite disastrous. The only thing seemed to be to contrive some way of doing it without your knowledge.

"Now, I realized that that was bound to be self-defeating in the end. There must come a time when you would notice it yourselves, and when other people would notice it, and start putting two and two together. But, with luck, it would still give me a number of years in hand. It did. It's getting on for ten years now since I gave Paul his first implant. Unfortunately, for all the progress I have been able to make, it might as well have been six months ago....

"So, there it is. I've done my best, and that hasn't been good enough. As for this business of Diana Brackley's, whether her particular emergency is really over, or not, doesn't greatly matter. It couldn't be so very long now until someone says: 'Strange how all three of those Saxovers look so young for their ages,' and sets someone else wondering about it. One day it'll start as simply as that—so it is perhaps time for you to know. All the same, it is best for everybody that it should be kept quiet as long as possible—something may yet turn up to make the crisis less critical, so we must give it all the time we can."

Zephanie did not speak for a little while, then she said:

"Daddy, what do you really feel about Diana and this?"

"Very complex, my dear."

"You seem to take that part of it so calmly—except when I told you about Nefertiti."

"I don't think I was ever very good at anti-climax. I'm sorry about the exhibition. As for the rest. Well, at first I was just plain angry. But I got over it. It was breach of contract, but it wasn't theft—I am satisfied about that. I've had nearly fifteen years to decide what to do with it—and I've failed. That, I think, is a fair enough allowance. Now, just what Diana has been doing I don't know, but she has had the sense to keep it quiet somehow. If she had not, it would have been tragic, but now . . . well, as I said, it can't last very much longer. No, I'm not angry—in several ways it's a relief not to be on one's own any longer. But I still want as much time as we can get before it breaks. . . ."

"If what Diana said is right—if she's got over the emergency safely—then things aren't really much different, are they?"

Francis shook his head.

"Three days ago I was on my own. Now I know that Diana knows, and we've doubled the number of people who actually do know."

"But it's only us, Daddy. Paul and me. Unless Diana has told someone . . . ?"

"She says not."

"There you are then. It's practically as-you-were."

Paul sat forward in his chair.

"That's all very well," he put in, "things may be the same for you, but they aren't for me. I have a wife."

His father and sister regarded him with little expression. He went on:

"As long as I didn't know—I didn't know. But now that I *do* know, well, as my wife she has a right to know, too."

The other two made no reply. Zephanie sat still, her hair gleaming against the dark leather of the chair back. She appeared to be interested in the pattern of the carpet. Francis did not meet his son's eye, either. The silence became awkward. It was Zephanie who broke it.

"You don't have to tell her at once, Paul. We need time to get used to the idea ourselves—to see it in proper perspective."

"You might try putting yourself in her place," Paul suggested. "What would you think of a husband who held out on you over a thing like this?"

"There aren't any things like this," Zephanie said. "It is a very particular and peculiar thing. I'm not saying you shouldn't tell her, but you can postpone it until we work out some kind of plan."

Paul said obstinately:

"She has a right to expect her husband to play square with her."

Zephanie turned to Francis.

"Tell him to wait a bit, Daddy—until we've had a chance to grasp what it's really going to mean."

Francis did not respond immediately. He polished the bowl of his pipe in his hand, regarded it thoughtfully for some moments, and then raised his eyes to meet his son's.

"This," he said, "is just what has hung over me for fourteen years. I told no one because I had no confidant I could really trust—never since your mother died.

"Once an idea has been planted no one can tell when and where it will stop growing. The only safe way of controlling it is not to plant it, not to give it a chance to germinate, I thought. That, it seems, was even wiser than I knew." He glanced up at the clock.

"It is now about three and a half hours since I let the idea out of its pod—since I confided it to you. Already it has germinated, and is struggling to grow. . . ."

He paused, and then went on:

"If I could appeal simply to cool reason I don't think we should be in difficulty. Unfortunately, however, husbands are seldom reasonable about wives, and wives are even less reasonable about husbands. You must not think I don't see your problem.

"Nevertheless, I shall say this: if you are willing to risk responsibility for precipitating a disaster on a scale you have never imagined, you will go ahead and do what seems to you the gentlemanly thing; but if you are wise you will tell no one, no one at all."

"And yet," said Paul, "you have just implied that if Mother had still been alive you would have confided in her."

Francis made no reply to that. He continued to regard his son steadily. Paul's expression became a little pinched.

"All right. I understand. You don't need to say anything," he told them harshly. "I'm quite aware that you never really liked Jane, either of you. Now you're telling me that you don't trust her. That's what it amounts to, isn't it?"

Zephanie made a slight movement as though she were about to speak, but changed her mind. Francis, too, said nothing.

Paul got up. Without looking at them again, he left the room, slamming the door behind him. A few moments later they heard a car pass on its way down the drive.

"I did not manage that well," Francis said. "I suppose he will tell her?"

"I'm afraid so, Daddy. And he *has* got a point, you know. Besides, he's scared stiff of the way it would take her if she were to find out that he had known, and *not* told her."

"Then what?" asked Francis.

"I imagine she'll come to you, wanting lichenin treatment for herself. I don't imagine she'll blurt it out—not yet."

Francis's only comment was a slow nod. After a little silence, Zephanie added:

"Daddy. Before I go, I'd like to know a little more about it, and what it's going to mean to me, please . . ."

5

Zephanie stepped out of the lift looking down into her bag, and fumbling for the key of her flat. A large figure rose from a severe-looking chair, which was intended rather to take the bareness off the landing than to be actually sat upon. He confronted her as she approached her door. Her expression shifted from abstraction, through recognition and recollection, to dismay, in one swift move.

"Oh, dear!" she said, inadequately.

"Oh dear, indeed," replied the young man, grimly. "Practically one hour ago I was to call for you. And I did."

"I'm terribly sorry, Richard. I am really . . ."

"But you just happened to forget all about it."

"Oh, I didn't, Richard—at least, I remembered this morning. But there's been such a lot since then. It—well, it went out of my mind."

"Indeed," Richard Treverne said again. He stood there, a tall, rather fair, burly young man, looking at her carefully, somewhat mollified by the genuineness of her confusion. "Such a lot of what?" he inquired.

"Family things," Zephanie explained vaguely. She put a hand on his lapel. "Please don't be angry, Richard. I couldn't help it. I had to go down home suddenly. It was one of those things. I'm terribly sorry . . ." She hunted in her bag again, and found the key.

"Come in and sit down. Give me just ten minutes to bath and change, and I'll be ready."

He grunted as he followed her in.

"Ten minutes'll make it just about five minutes after the curtain has gone up. *If* it *is* ten minutes."

She paused, looking at him uncertainly.

"Oh, Richard. Would you mind dreadfully if we didn't? Couldn't we just go and have dinner somewhere quiet? I know it's piggish of me, but I couldn't enjoy the theater tonight. . . . Perhaps if you ring them up they'll be able to get rid of the seats. . . ."

He regarded her a little more attentively.

"Family rows? Someone died?" he inquired.

She shook her head.

"Just a bit of a shock. It'll pass—if you'll help to make it pass, Richard."

"All right," he agreed. "I'll ring them. No need to worry, then—except that I'm getting hungry."

She put her hand on his sleeve, and lifted her face for a kiss. "Darling Richard," she said, and made off toward her bedroom.

After this poorish start, the evening did not recover well. Zephanie tried artificial aid to lighten it. She had two martinis before they left the flat, and another two at the restaurant. Finding these ineffective she insisted that nothing but a fizzy wine would restore her spirits—which, though in a way that troubled Richard, it appeared to do, for a time. At the end of the meal her demands for a double brandy were so insistent that he overrode his judgment and ordered it. With that, the wine mood collapsed. She became weepy, and sniffed, and demanded more brandy. At his refusal, she felt miserably hard done by, and appealed tearfully to the charity of the head-waiter, who presently helped to maneuver her protestant departure with impressive tact.

Back at the flat, Richard helped her out of her coat, and stowed her in a corner of the sitting-room sofa where she curled up, weeping gently to herself. He went along to the little kitchen, and set a kettle to boil. Presently he returned with a jug of strong, black coffee.

"Go on. The whole cup," he told her as she paused.

"No. You mustn't bully, Richard."

"Yes," he insisted, and stood over her until she finished it.

Then she leaned back into the corner of the sofa again. The weeping had finished, leaving her face remarkably unravaged. Eyes still bright, their rims a little pink, but the rest had cleared without trace, as a child's face can. And indeed, he thought, gazing at her, that was what it was: a child's face. It was difficult to believe, as she sat there twisting her handkerchief and disconsolately avoiding his eyes, that she was more than seventeen.

"Now then," he said warmly. "What's it all about? What's the trouble?"

She shook her head, without replying.

"Don't be an ass," he told her kindly. "People like you don't go and get tight deliberately for no reason. And people who make a habit of it need a lot more than you've had."

"Richard! Are you saying I'm tight?" she demanded, with an attempt at dignity.

"Yes. And you are. Drink another cup of this coffee," he told her.

"No!"

"Yes," he insisted.

Sulkily she drank half.

"Now, let's have it," he said.

"No. It's a secret," said Zephanie.

"To hell with that. I can keep secrets. How can I help you if I don't know what the trouble is?"

"Can't help me. Nobody can help. 'S a secret," she said.

"It often helps just to talk about things," Richard told her.

She looked at him, long, and fairly steadily. Her eyes glistened, brimmed, and began to overflow again.

"Oh, God!" said Richard. He hesitated, then moved across and sat down beside her on the sofa. He took her hand.

"Look, Zeph, darling," he told her, "things often seem the wrong size when you're up against them all by yourself. Let's have it out, whatever it is, and see what we can do. This way of going on isn't you at all, Zephie."

She clung to his hand, and the tears trickled down.

"I'm f-frightened, Richard. I don't want it. I don't want it."

"You don't want what?" he asked blankly, looking at her helplessly.

She shook her head.

Suddenly his whole attitude stiffened. He stared at her bleakly for some moments, then:

"Oh!" he said very flatly. After a pause he added:

"And you only knew today?"

"This morning," she told him. "But I didn't really—well, I mean, it just seemed sort of exciting at first."

"Oh," he said again.

There was a silence which stretched out for almost a minute. Then he turned suddenly, and took her by the shoulders.

"Oh, God, Zephie . . . Oh, Zeph darling . . . Why couldn't you wait for me?"

Zephanie looked back at him, bemused, and still woeful.

"Richard, darling," she said, mournfully.

"Who was it?" he demanded fiercely. "Just tell me who it was and I'll—I'll . . . Who did it?"

"Why, Daddy, of course," Zephanie said. "He meant it for the best," she added, loyally.

Richard's jaw dropped. His arms, too. For a moment or two he looked as if he had been hit on the head by a mallet. He needed an appreciable time to rally. At last:

"We don't appear to be thinking about the same thing," he remarked with grim restraint. "Let's get it clear. What *is* this whatever-it-is that you so passionately don't want?"

"Oh, Richard, don't be unkind," she said, miserably.

"Damn it, I'm not being unkind. I've had a shock, too. Now I just want to know what the hell we're talking about, that's all."

She stared at him, not quite focused.

"Why, about me, of course. About me, and going on and on and on. Jus' think of it, Richard. Everybody getting old and tired and dying, and jus' me going on and on and on, all alone, on and on and on. It doesn't seem exciting now, Richard, I'm frightened. I want to die like other people. Not on and on—jus' love and live and grow old and die. That's all I want to do." She ended, with the tears flowing fast again.

Richard regarded her attentively.

"Now you've reached the morbid stage," he said.

"It *is* morbid—just going on and on and on. Very morbid," she asserted.

He told her firmly:

"That's enough of this on and on nonsense, Zeph. It's time you packed it in, and got to bed. Try consoling yourself by thinking of the sadder side—'In the morning it is green and groweth up: but in the evening it is cut down, dried up, and withered.' For my part I prefer a bit of on and on, and leaving the drying up and withering as long as possible."

"But two hundred years is too much on and on and on, *I* think. Such a long, long way to go all alone, all alone. Two hundred years is—" She stopped abruptly, looking at him wide-eyed. "Oh dear! shouldn't have said that. You mus' forget it, Richard. 'S a secret. Most important secret, Richard."

"All right, Zephie, dear. It's safe with me. Now you get along to bed."

"Can't. You help me there, Richard."

He picked her up, carried her to the bedroom, and laid her on the bed. Her arms clinched firmly round his neck.

"You stay," she said. "Stay with me. Please, Richard."

He struggled to detach the arms.

"You're tight, darling. Just you relax and go to sleep. You'll be all right in the morning."

Tears came again.

"But I'm so lonely, Richard. I'm frightened. All alone. You'll be dead, everybody dead—'cept me, going on and on and on."

Richard succeeded in disentangling himself. He put her arms down firmly. She turned her head, and wept into her pillow. He stood for a moment at the bedside, then he bent down and kissed her gently below her ear.

Leaving the door of her room a little ajar, he went back to the sitting-room and lit a cigarette. Even before it was finished, the sound of sobs had ebbed, and then ceased. He gave her a few minutes more before he tiptoed back. The sound of her breathing did not falter as he switched off the light.

He closed her door softly, collected his hat and coat, and let himself out of the flat.

—

Telling Jane turned out to be less simple than Paul had thought. To start with, he had forgotten that they were invited that evening to a cocktail party by which she set some store. His late arrival home was met with chilly reproof; his suggestion that they should skip the party was curtly rejected. Then the party itself, with the unsatisfying support of something called a fork-supper, lasted all the evening. A final snack at home with which they supplemented the deficiencies of the fork-supper did not offer the ideal occasion for an announcement of major importance. So he decided to wait until they were in bed. But Jane snuggled down with the air of one determined to sleep. Paul turned out the light. He toyed for a moment with the idea of making his announcement into the darkness, but then, out of experience, thought better of it. While he was still not quite decided, her breathing became regular, and that settled the matter. Revelation must be postponed until next day.

Jane's character had been worked upon by forces and circumstances which had barely touched the Saxover, and the most important of these was financial stress, for, while in the Saxover family money was a by-product which seemed to increase almost of itself, the concern of her own family for as long as she could remember had been the rate at which it dwindled.

Her father, Colonel Parton, regular army, retired, held a small estate in Cumberland; the kind of estate that had been pared away piece by piece until the little of it that remained could now well be in its last generation as a family seat. The Colonel's only son, Henry, by a former marriage, was a presentable and, indeed, popular young man. There had been hopes that he might marry well, but he had dashed these by espousing the rector's daughter, thus disposing of the last chance that he might become a scion capable of beating the fiscal vultures off his father's corpse.

Reluctantly facing this fact, the Colonel had transferred his final hopes to his daughter, for, even now, it is not impossible for a dutiful daughter, capably instructed in the hard facts of life, to prove an asset. And if she shows aptitude it is worth raising some capital to back her—might just as well take the chance, anyway: no good trying to save, with the Chancellor of the Exchequer waiting there at the end of the line like a figure of doom. So the capital had been invested in an expensive school, a Paris finishing, a London season, and had culminated, after several rather more glamorous frustrations, in marriage to Paul.

Though Jane was not exactly what Francis would have wished for his son, and it could scarcely fail to occur to him that the Saxover prospects had played some part in her decision, he recalled earlier possibilities that would have pleased him less, and put a good face on it. As well as looks, Jane had assurance. Her manner and appearance were precisely those expected of a young woman in her stratum. Her social instincts were well developed, her sense of taboo was reliable, and she had a proper respect for all of the Commandments that were currently in good standing. There could be little doubt of her capacity to be a most presentable wife, and a capable manager. Also, she knew what she was doing, and where she intended to go—and that, with certain reservations, was to the good, Francis felt. Certainly a clinger would not have been suitable for Paul.

Nevertheless, Paul had been right when he said that neither his father nor his sister liked Jane. Both had tried. Francis was prepared to go on trying, but Zephanie had given up.

"I'm sorry, Daddy," she had admitted to Francis. "I've done my best, but she and I don't seem to live in the same world, or see the same things at all. She doesn't think about anything—she's sort of programmed, like a computer. There's a conditioned response system. She hears, and then acceptance, rejection, and reaction drums go click-click-click, and the answer comes out sort of codified, just exactly right for people who use the same code."

"Isn't that a little intolerant?" Francis had suggested. "After all, aren't we all rather like that if we consider ourselves honestly?"

"To some degree," Zephanie admitted. "Only some people seem to be rigged always to pay the house—like fruit machines."

Francis had rested a speculative eye on his daughter.

"I think perhaps we had better drop this analogy," he said.

"But I trust that we shall do our best to preserve a civilized relationship in the family."

"Of course," Zephanie agreed, and then added as an afterthought: "Though that's really just it—'civilized' is one of those words that she decodes quite differently from you and me."

Thereafter, Zephanie had followed a course of measured disengagement from her sister-in-law's society, which suited both parties.

And that, Paul thought, as he reconsidered his approach, wasn't going to make Jane's reception of the news any kindlier.

Morning was not, he realized, the ideal time to broach the subject. On the other hand, they were going out again that evening, so he would be in the same position tomorrow, and he was aware that the longer he delayed, the stronger Jane's position would be. In the end, he decided in favor of the direct move: over his second cup of coffee he came straight at it.

There is no conventional reply provided for a young woman whose husband tells her across the breakfast table, and in a rather explosive way, that he expects to live for two hundred years.

What Jane Saxover did do was, first, to stare at him blankly, then, to rally her faculties in order to examine his countenance more carefully. Much of it was hidden by beard, but it is chiefly the eyes that are important at such times. She sought in them a poached look, off-color whites, a clenching of the surrounding muscles, and found none of these things. Negative evidence, however, was not enough; a wife naturally feels easier when an aberration can be ascribed to a traditional cause, and the more hackneyed the cause, the happier. Even the fact that she had not noticed anything amiss the previous night was hopefully disregarded. She affected not to have heard properly, giving him an opportunity to reconsider his announcement, without loss of face on either side.

"Well," she said consideringly, "expectation of life *has* increased a lot in the last fifty years. Perhaps living to a hundred won't be anything very remarkable in another generation or so."

It is frustrating to have one's dramatic swipe parried by a cushion. Paul replied irritably.

"I didn't say a hundred years," he told her. "I said *two* hundred years."

She inspected him again.

"Paul, are you feeling quite well? I did warn you not to mix them last night. It never agrees with you—"

Paul's customary consideration lapsed.

"Oh God, the banality of women!" he exclaimed. "I drove you home, didn't I? Haven't you got two bits of imagination to rub together?"

Jane started to get up from the table.

"If you are going to be abusive—"

"Sit down!" he snapped at her. "And stop giving me standard reactions and standard phrases. Sit down, and listen. What I've got to tell you affects *you*."

Jane was aware that by the unwritten handbook of strategy and tactics this was the moment when withdrawal would leave the opposing forces in a state of bafflement and deteriorating morale. On the other hand, Paul did look genuinely anxious about something, and was unlike his usual self, so she hesitated.

When he shouted "Sit down" again, she did so, more from surprise than from anything else.

"Now," said Paul, "if you will listen, and suspend the series of reflex discounts for a while, you'll find that what I have to say is of considerable importance."

Jane listened. At the end of it, she said:

"But Paul, you really can't expect me to believe this. It's fantastic. Your father must be joking."

Paul's fingers tensed. He glared at her in a quite alarming way, then he relaxed.

"Evidently they were right," he said wearily. "I'd have done better not to mention it."

"Who were right?"

"Why, Father and Zephanie, of course."

"You mean to say they told you not to tell me?"

"They did. But what's it matter? It's all a joke. You said so."

"You mean it isn't a joke?"

"Oh, for God's sake! A—you've surely known my father long enough to know it's not the kind of thing he'd joke about, and B—a joke is meant to be humorous. And if you can tell me anything humorous about this, I'd like to hear it."

"But why didn't they want me to hear about it?"

"It wasn't exactly that. They wanted me to postpone telling you until there's a course of action worked out."

"Although I'm your wife, and a member of the family?"

"Well, damn it, the old man never even told Zephanie and me until yesterday."

"But surely you must have guessed. How long has it been going on?"

"Since I was seventeen, and with Zeph since she was sixteen."

"And you expect me to believe that in ten years you never guessed?"

"Well, *you* wouldn't believe it when I told you flat, would you? Hang it, one may guess at a few things which seem to be possibilities, but what the devil would be the good of going about guessing over all the *im*possibilities? All that happened was this. . . ."

He explained about his father's concocted story of the new immunization treatment, ending:

"It healed up quickly, leaving just a bit of a bump under the skin, and that's all there was to it. We've repeated it each year since. How was I to know that it wasn't just what he said?"

Jane regarded him dubiously.

"But there must have been some effects. Didn't you notice *anything?*"

"Yes," said Paul. "I noticed that I don't take colds very easily. I've had flu only twice, and mildly, in ten years. And that my cuts and scratches seldom fester. I noticed that because it was the kind of thing I was looking for. Why should I look for anything else?"

Jane let that go for the moment.

"Why two hundred years? Why so definite?" she asked.

"Because that's the way it works. I don't know the details yet, and I'd very likely not understand them, anyway, but what he told us is, roughly, that it slows down the rate of cell division and the whole metabolism to one-third of normal—which means that since it started I only get one year older in every three years that pass."

Jane's eyes dwelled on him thoughtfully.

"I see. So now your actual age is twenty-seven, your physical age is just over twenty. Is that what you mean?"

Paul nodded. "That's how I understand it."

"But you never noticed a little thing like that?"

"Of course I noticed that I look young for my age—that's why I grew this beard. But plenty of other people look young for their age, too."

Jane looked skeptically at him.

"What are you up to?" he inquired. "Trying to persuade yourself that I was holding out on you? Now we *know,* of course we can see the evidence. Why, damn it, haven't you yourself remarked how infrequently I need a haircut, and what a devil of a time my beard took to grow, and how seldom my nails need trimming? Why didn't *you* deduce it from that?"

"Well," said Jane thoughtfully, "even if you didn't guess Zephanie must have done."

"I don't see why she should, any more than I. Less, in fact; she doesn't have to shave," Paul replied.

"Darling," Jane told him, using the word edge uppermost, "you don't have to pretend to be dim with me."

"I don't—oh, I see what you mean," Paul said. "All the same, I don't think she did guess. There wasn't any sign of it. Though she was a bit quicker on the uptake than me."

"She *must* have guessed," Jane repeated. "She goes down to Darr quite a lot. And even if she didn't guess she must have heard from somebody who would naturally think she knew about it."

"But I've told you," Paul said patiently. "*Nobody else* did know—at least, he thought not until this cropped up."

Jane thought for some little time. Finally she shook her head.

"How ingenuous can you be? Paul, I don't believe you've even begun to consider what this implies. It's worth millions—millions of millions. There are hundreds of men and women who would be willing to pay thousands a year to have their lives extended like that. It's a thing that all the wealth of all the richest men in history hasn't been able to buy before. Now, are you really expecting me to believe that your father has done simply *nothing* with it in fourteen years—except treat you two? For heaven's sake, show a little common sense, Paul!"

"But you don't understand. That's not the point at all. Oh, I don't say there isn't fame, and probably a great deal of money for him eventually. But that's not what's concerning him at the moment—why should it? Part of the thing *is* that it gives him lots of time to play with. He—"

Jane interrupted suddenly.

"Do you mean to say he's been treating himself?"

"Naturally. You don't think he'd try it on us without satisfying himself about it first, do you?"

"But—" Jane's hand on the table was clenched so that the knuckles were white, "—do you mean he's going to live to be two hundred, too?" she demanded tensely.

"Well, not as long as that, of course. He started it later in life."

"But he *could* go on to be more than a hundred?"

"Oh, easily I should think."

Jane regarded her husband. She opened her mouth to pursue this line of thought, but hesitated, and decided against it for the moment.

Paul went on:

"The thing at present is that he can't see how to put it across—how it can be introduced with the least possible dislocation."

Jane said:

"Well, *I* really can't see much trouble about that. Just show me any rich man who wouldn't give him a fortune for the treatment—*and* the man would keep it confidential in his own interests. What's more, I'll bet that's what several of them are doing."

"Implying that my father is behaving like a kind of super-quack?"

"Oh, rubbish! He is a shrewd businessman over his contracts—you've always said that yourself. So, I ask you, what man of business ability is going to let an opportunity like this lie idle for fourteen years? It just doesn't make sense."

"So because this isn't a thing you can put on the market like a detergent—it follows that he must be doing it hole-in-corner?"

"What's the *use* of it if it isn't put on the market somehow or other? Sooner or later it's bound to be. Obviously the only thing to be gained by not putting it on the open market at once is the high value you can put on carefully restricted sales. And how high! Give anyone convincing proof, and he'd beg you to take half his capital for it." She paused, and went on:

"And where do you come in? He goes on with it for all this time, and you don't hear a thing until there's a leak somewhere, and he reckons the best of it's over, and you're likely to find out anyway, so then he tells you.

"He must have been making millions out of this—and just kept it all to himself.... *And* he's given himself a new lease of life. How long is it going to be before any of it comes to us—a century or so?"

Paul looked at his wife uneasily. It was his turn to hesitate and change his mind. Catching his expression, she said:

"There's nothing wrong with facing facts. It's natural for old people to die, and for younger people to inherit."

Paul did not take that up. He reverted:

"But you've got it all *wrong*," he repeated. "If he wanted to be fabulously rich he wouldn't be as he is—Darr wouldn't be run as he runs it, in fact it would never have existed. His overriding interest is his work, and it always has been. It's the consequences that are worrying him. As for suggesting that he'd ever go about launching it like some back-street abortionist—it's just damned nonsense. You must know him better than that."

"Every man has his price—" Jane began.

"I daresay, but it isn't always money."

"If it isn't, it's power," said Jane. "Money is power. Enough money is infinite power, so it comes to the same thing."

"And he isn't a megalomaniac, either. He's just a very worried man, worried stiff about the effects of this thing. If you were to talk to him—"

"*If!*" she repeated. "My dear Paul, I have every intention of talking to him. I have quite a lot to say to him—starting with an inquiry as to why we have been excluded from the scheme until it shows signs of falling apart. And not only that. You don't seem to realize what he has been doing to me—your wife, his own daughter-in-law. *If* all this you say is true, then he has quite deliberately let me get two years older when it need only have been eight months. He has cold-bloodedly cheated me of sixteen months of life I could have had. What have you to say to that ... ?"

6

"I'd like to have a go at it. There's something there worth looking into. Sure of it," said Gerald Marlin.

"Very U outfit, Nefertiti. Got to be damn sure of your footholds," responded the editor of the *Sunday Prole.*

"Naturally. But just the kind of outfit our readers would enjoy seeing socked. High-class luxury scandal stuff."

"M'm," said the editor dubiously.

"Look, Bill," Gerald insisted. "This Wilberry woman has shaken 'em down for five thousand. Five thousand—and she'd have been lucky to get five hundred if it had gone to court. They cut her down, of course. Her first bid was ten thousand. You can't say that doesn't stink."

"Classy joints like that will pay a lot to keep out of the courts. Wrong kind of publicity."

"But five thousand!"

"Just an item on expenses, the Treasury pays." He paused. "Frankly, Gerald, I doubt whether there's anything in it. The Wilberry woman just happens to have an allergy. Could happen to anyone. Frequently does. Shaking down the hair-dye people for it used to be popular at one time. God knows what they put into all the creams, lotions, rinses and what-have-you's that they use in those places. Anything could happen. Suppose you were allergic to whales."

"If I were allergic to whales, or whale-oil, I'd not have to go to a high-priced beauty-pusher to find out."

"What I mean is if someone comes along and says: 'Here is Science's latest Homage to Beauty! Imperial Goo—rarest of Nature's gifts—is found only during June in the left ventricle of the hunting-wasp whence it is extracted drop by precious drop by expert scientists dedicated to giving YOU new beauty!' Well, how are you going to know whether you are allergic to this particular muck or not, until you've tried it? Most people will be okay, anyway, but every now and then up pops the one in a hundred thousand who sort of fizzes on contact with it. If too many come over funny you have to think up a new kind of goo, but a few here and there are just a trade hazard—and the Wilberry woman happens to be one of them. She's a calculated risk, like ullage and so on, but naturally they don't want publicity, if they can help it."

"Yes, but—"

"I don't think you realize what the takings are in a stratospheric dump like that, old boy—with all the etceteras. I'd be surprised if it averages out at much under three hundred per annum per client."

"We're obviously in the wrong business, Bill. But all the same there's something fishy somewhere. That Wilberry woman would gladly have settled for three, or even two, but her solicitors held out for five, and got it. There has to be a reason— And it isn't dope— At least, Scotland Yard's found no evidence of that; they keep quite an eye on these places, you know."

"Well, if they're satisfied—"

"So if it's not dope, it's something else."

"Even so, all these places have what they like to think of as valuable trade secrets—though God knows why all women aren't raving beauties if there's anything in them."

"All right, then, suppose it is just a trade secret—it's built up one hell of a successful high-class business, so why shouldn't we try to winkle it out, and *give* it to our readers?"

The editor pondered.

"You may have something there," he admitted.

"I'm sure I have. There's *something*. Whether it's funny business, or a first-class beauty recipe doesn't greatly matter—we could run either."

They contemplated the prospect for a few moments.

"Besides," Gerald went on, "there's something about this Brackley woman who runs it. Not the type. Real brains, apparently—not just the usual business cunning, I mean. I've got a bit of preliminary dope on her."

He felt in his pocket, produced a couple of folded sheets of paper and handed them across.

The editor unfolded them. They were headed: "Diana Priscilla Brackley—Preliminary" and had been rattled through a typewriter by someone more concerned with speed than precision. Disregarding the mis-spellings, mishits, and doing his best with erratic contractions, the editor read:

"D. P. Brackley, aged 39, but said to look much younger (will check whether fact or polite fiction, may be trade asset). A looker. Five foot ten, dark red-brown hair, good features, gray eyes. Drives a heck of a fine Rolls—cost, say, seven thousand. Lives 83 Darlington Mansions, sw1—rent astronomical.

"Father Harold Brackley dead, bank-clerk, Wessex Bank Ltd, exemplary, staunch member bank's Repertory Company. Married Malvina, second daughter Valentine de Travers, wealthy works contractor, by elopement. V. de T. heavy father—never darken door, not a penny from me, etc.

"Brackleys lived 43 Despent Road, Clapham, semi-detached, small mortgage. Subject, only child. Local private school until 11. Then St. Merryn's High School. Did well. Outstanding scholarship Cambridge. Honours, distinctions with bells on. Biochemistry. Took job three and a half years Darr House Developments, Ockinham.

"Meanwhile V. de T. died. Daughter and son-in-law still unforgiven, but bequest to grand-daughter, Subject, believed to be between forty and fifty thousand, at age twenty-five. Subject turned in Darr House job six months after that age. (Note: *After* appears to be typical. V. level headed.) Commissioned building of house for parents near Ashford, Kent. Took round-world tour—one year.

"On return bought into small beauty-business The Freshet, Mayfair somewhere. Two years later bought out partner. Next year absorbed her Freshet into the new Nefertiti Ltd (private: nom. capital £100). Has gone ahead beautifying the knobs of the nobs ever since, and not half.

"Personal details scanty—in spite of scandalling habit of the trade. No marriages as far as known yet—certainly has kept maiden name throughout. Lives costly, but not flashy. Spends freely on dress. No known sidelines—though has an interest in Joynings, manufacturing chemists. No funny business known. Seems straight. Business reputation exemplary clean. All Nefertiti staff carefully vetted, no smudged characters accepted. Too good to be true? Think not. Just v. careful to maintain repute. Even bitchy rivals' detractions insubstantial.

"Love-life: no public knowledge. Seems none current, or recent, but research proceeds."

"H'm," said the editor as he reached the end. "No very *human* figure emerges, does it?"

"That's just a rough preliminary," Gerald said. "He'll get more. *I* think it's interesting. That Darr House job, for instance. They only have the bright ones there—it's practically the equivalent of putting letters after your name to get taken on. So I ask myself what makes anyone of that caliber come out of higher egghead researches, and get into the age-old flummery of the beauty-racket?"

"On the face of it, the desire to run a Rolls-Royce—with appropriate ensembles," suggested his editor.

Gerald shook his head.

"Not good enough, Bill. If cutting a dash were the motive, she'd be a lot better known than she is. The really big beauty-peddlers like to queen it as a rule—part of the publicity. Look at it this way. She, an outsider of a different type altogether, goes into the pulchritude jostle, all among the vitriol throwers and smilers with knives, and what happens? She not only survives, but she makes a success, a real classy success, there, and apparently without adopting the local weapons. How? There's only one answer to that, Bill—a gimmick. She has something that the others haven't got. Considering the report I'd say that as a scientific worker she came across something when she was at the Darr House place, and decided to cash in on it. Whether it's shady, or not, is a different matter—but I reckon it's worth finding out."

His editor continued to muse. Then he nodded.

"All right, Gerry, boy, you look into it. But go canny. The Nefertiti outfit packs a lot of high-powered feminine influence. *If* you find anything that's going to blow up into a big scandal there'd be some important wives involved. So just bear that in mind, will you?"

———

"I'll tell madam you are here, Miss," said the little maid and departed, closing the door behind her.

The room had clung to simplicities eschewing ornamentation in a way that made it slightly old-fashioned to Zephanie's eyes, even somewhat stark, by modern standards, but it was an expensive, tasteful kind of starkness, and, after the first surprise, not unpleasing. Zephanie walked over to the window. Beyond it, and accessible by a half-glassed door, some square yards of roof were laid out as a small garden. Dwarf tulips were in bloom in several beds. On a bank in the shade of carefully clipped bushes a few violets grew. In one corner of a miniature lawn a tiny fountain played in an antique lead spout-head. Large sheets of glass coming up out of slots in a low wall screened it from the wind on one side. In front, one gazed westward over a small wrought-iron fence, across the park which seemed all newly green tree-tops, to the misty outlines of buildings beyond.

"Gosh!" said Zephanie, in honest envy.

At the sound of the door opening, she turned. Diana stood there in a simple, beautifully cut, gray silk suit. Her only ornaments were a plain gold bracelet on her wrist, a gold pin on her lapel, and a flexible gold necklet.

For some moments they looked at one another without speaking.

Diana was almost exactly as Zephanie remembered her. She must, she knew, be very nearly forty now; she looked—well, perhaps twenty-eight, certainly no more. Zephanie smiled, with a touch of uncertainty.

"This makes me feel like a little girl again," she said.

Diana smiled back.

"You still only just manage to look like a bigger girl now," she told Zephanie.

They went on looking at one another.

"It *is* true. It really does work," Zephanie murmured, half to herself.

"You have only to look in a mirror," said Diana.

"That's not quite enough. It might be simply me. But you—you're just as lovely, Diana—and no older at all."

Diana took both her hands, and then put one arm round her.

"It's been a bit of a shock, I suspect," she said.

Zephanie nodded.

"It was rather, at first," she admitted. "I felt so terribly *alone* with it. I'm getting over that now, though."

"You sounded a bit tense on the telephone. I thought it would be best to meet here where we can talk," Diana explained. "But we'll come to that. First, I want to hear what's been happening to you, and to your father, and all about Darr, too."

They talked. Diana gradually smoothed away Zephanie's nervousness and the sense of unreality that had been overhanging her. By the time luncheon was over she felt more at ease than she had at any time since Francis had sprung his news. Back in the sitting-room, however, Diana steered round to the reason for her call.

"Well now, what do you want me to do, my dear? What's the trouble?—From your angle, I mean."

Zephanie said, uncertainly:

"You've done some of it already. You've reassured me. I'd got to feeling I was a kind of freak—I don't know. But I do want to understand what's going on. I'm in such a muddle. Here's Daddy made a discovery that's going to—to, well, sort of ring down the ages. I mean, it'll make him like Newton, and Jenner, and Einstein, won't it? And instead of being acclaimed as a wonderful discoverer he's gone all hole-in-corner. And then he thinks he's the only one who knows, and it turns out you've known about it all the time—but you've kept it quiet, too. I don't understand. I know Daddy says there isn't enough of the lichenin to do much with, but that's very often so with a new thing. Once it's *known* to be possible it's half the battle: everybody starts researching madly, and people come up with alternative methods. After all, if there isn't much of that actual lichen it can't do so very much harm, so why not publish, and give people the incentive to find another antigerone, as he calls it? So then I began to wonder if there are some side-effects, things like—well, if you have lichenin you can't have babies, or something of that kind."

"You can set your mind at rest over that, at any rate," Diana assured her. "It makes no difference—only, naturally, you don't want to gestate like an elephant, so you lay off the lichenin, and return to normal rate. As for other side-effects, there aren't any hidden ones that I know. There's an infinitesimal slowing of the response rate just detectable by measurement, less than you get after one double gin. The rest are obvious—to yourself, that is."

"Good," said Zephanie, "that's one worry less. But, Diana, I feel in the half-dark about the whole thing. I mean, where you came into it, and about Nefertiti and the beauty business, and this crisis that blew up and then disappeared, and so on."

Diana reached for a cigarette, rapped it, and regarded it thoughtfully for a moment.

"All right," she said. "Half-knowledge is precarious, anyway. I'd better begin at the beginning." She lit a cigarette, and started from the time Francis brought in the saucer of milk, and the consequences.

"So, legally," she concluded, "I'm in the wrong, though morally I've just as much right to it as your father has, but never mind about that now. The point is that where both of us got stuck was the handling of it. It took me some time to realize how stuck I was. I thought I'd soon see a way out, but then the more I thought about it the more difficulties there were. And it was only then that I began to understand just how important it was.

"I couldn't see a way of dealing with it at all—and then something you said suddenly put me on the track."

"Something I said?" Zephanie repeated.

"Yes. We were talking about women being diddled, you remember?"

"I remember. It was rather a theme of yours," Zephanie said, with a smile.

"It still is," Diana told her. "But that time you said you'd mentioned it to one of your teachers, and she'd said we must do our best to live in the circumstances we found because life was too short to put the world to rights, or words to that effect."

"I'm not sure that I do remember that."

"Well, that was the gist of it. Of course it had been in my mind all along, in a way. What we've really found, your father and I, is a step in evolution, a kind of synthetic evolution—and the *only* evolutionary advance by man in a million years. It is going to change the whole of future history completely. Oh yes, I'd realized that if life weren't so short it would be worth people's while to do more to put the world to rights. But, when you said it as you did, I suddenly saw, in a kind of flash, how it could be put across."

"Put across?" Zephanie said in a bewildered tone.

"Yes. I saw how women could be started on longer lives without even knowing it, at first. Later on, they would find out, and by that time I hoped there would be enough of them, and enough of the right kind, to wield real influence. What was necessary was somehow to collect a group of people—any group of people—convince them that extended life was practicable, and make them *fight* for the acceptance of *homo superior*. And, suddenly, I saw how to do it. People who have been given long-life are not going to renounce it. They are going to fight hard for their right to retain it."

Zephanie frowned a little.

"I don't think I quite follow," she said.

"You should do," Diana told her. "You feel a bit confused and upset now, but you wouldn't exactly go to the length of renouncing a longer life, would you? And you'd maintain your right to it if anyone wanted to take it away, wouldn't you?"

"Yes—I suppose so. But there's the shortage of supply . . ."

"Oh, research will soon clear that up, as you said yourself, once there is the demand. Get enough money to put enough people on the job, that's all."

"But according to Daddy there'll be a state of chaos."

"Of course there'll be chaos. We shan't get *homo superior* without any birth-pangs. But that's not important. What *is* important is to stop him being strangled at birth. *That's* the problem."

"I just don't see that. Once it's known about, people will be fighting to get it and have longer lives."

"You're talking about individuals, my dear, but individuals are subject to institutions. And the crux of the whole thing is, as I see it, that institutions will very definitely *not* want it.

"After all, most institutions have two main reasons for existence; one is to make large scale administration possible, the other is to preserve continuity, and so dodge some of the difficulties which arise from the shortness of our individual lives. Our institutions are a product of our circumstances, and they are designed to survive our own limitations by continual replacement of worn-out parts, or, if you prefer a different view, by a system of promotion.

"All right? Very well, then, now try asking yourself how many people are going to favor the prospect of long life at the cost of, say, two or three hundred years as an underling? Is anybody going to welcome the thought of the same managing director, president, judge, ruler, party-leader, pope, police-chief, or leading dressmaker going on for a couple of centuries? You think it over, and you'll see that institutions are what they are, and as they are, because behind them all is the assumption that the days of our age are threescore years and ten, or thereabouts. Take that away, and they won't work, most of them will even lose their whole *raison d'être.*"

"That's very sweeping," Zephanie said doubtfully.

"You think it over. Just take an example. You are a junior grade civil servant; of course you'd like a longer life—until you realize that it means polishing your pants on that same junior grade seat for the next fifty or sixty years: then you're not quite so sure.

"Or you are one of those little girls who rush lemming-like into marriage at the first chance—well, the death-do-us-part view is beginning to wear pretty thin even now; I don't think it's going to stand up at all well to the prospect of a hundred and fifty years to be spent with a partner grabbed in adolescence.

"Or think of education. The sort of smattering that's been good enough to tide most of us over fifty years isn't going to give us a full life for two hundred, or more.

"So what we'll have is Individual Man in a life-and-death tussle with Institutional Man—and a fine crop of schizophrenia that ought to raise.

"And you can't make it a matter of personal choice, either, if only because any man who chooses long life would block any promotion of the men who did not.

"So, as institutions are greater than the sum of their parts, and everyone is a part of some social and professional institutions, it follows that institutions, working desperately to survive, would stand a good chance of bringing about the rejection of lichenin altogether."

Zephanie shook her head.

"Oh, no, I can't believe that. It's absolutely contrary to our natural survival instincts."

"That scarcely counts. All civilized behavior has had to suppress god knows how many instincts. I put the possibility of rejection very high indeed."

"But—well, even if there were official rejection, it would be made quite ineffective by hundreds of thousands of people privately flouting the law," Zephanie maintained.

"I'd not be at all sure of that, either. A small privileged class might try, at great expense. A sort of black-market longer life. But I can't see it working very well—scarcely the kind of illegality one could hide, is it?—not for long, anyway."

Zephanie turned toward the window. For some moments she watched the small sunlit clouds drifting in a blue sky.

"I came here still a bit frightened—for myself," she said. "But excited, too, because I thought I was beginning to understand that Daddy's discovery—well, yours and Daddy's discovery—was one of the greatest steps ever made; one of the oldest dreams come true; something that was going to change all history, and bring us into a wonderful new era. . . . But *he* thinks people will be fighting one another for it—and *you* think they'll be fighting one another to stop it, so what's the use? If it isn't going to bring anything but fighting and wretchedness, then it would be better if neither of you had ever found it."

Diana looked at her thoughtfully.

"You don't mean that, my dear. You know as well as I do that the world is in a mess, and floundering deeper every day. We have only a precarious hold on the forces we do liberate—and problems that we ought to be trying to solve, we neglect. Look at us—thousands more of us every day. . . . In a century or so, we shall be in the Age of Famines. We shall manage to postpone the worst one way and another, but postponement isn't solution, and when the breakdown comes there'll be something so ghastly that the hydrogen-bomb will seem humane by comparison.

"I'm not romancing. I'm talking about the inevitable time when, unless we do something to stop it, men will be hunting men through the ruins, for food. We're letting it drift toward that, with an evil irresponsibility, because with our ordinary short lives we shan't be here to see it. Does our generation care about the misery it is bequeathing? Not it. 'That's their worry,' we say. 'Damn our children's children; we're all right.'

"And there's only one thing I can see that will stop it happening. That is that some of us, at least, should be going to live long enough to be afraid of it for *ourselves.* And also that we should live long enough to *know* more. We simply cannot afford to go on any longer attaining wisdom only half a step before we achieve senility. We need the *time* to acquire wisdom that we can use to clear up the mess. If we don't get it, then like any other animal that overbreeds we shall starve; we shall starve in our millions, in the blackest of all dark ages.

"That's why we *need* longer life, before it is too late. To give us time to acquire the wisdom to control our destiny; to get us beyond this state of acting like animal prodigies, and let us civilize ourselves."

She broke off, and smiled ruefully at Zephanie.

"Sorry for the tub-thumping, my dear. It's such a relief to be able to say it to someone. All it really means is that however much chaos this may cause now, the alternative would be infinitely worse."

Zephanie made no reply for some minutes, then she said:

"Is this the way you saw it all that time ago when you were at Darr, Diana?"

Diana shook her head.

"No, this is how I've come to see it. In those days, I saw it as a gift we must use because it seemed to me to be, as I said, a step in evolution, a new development that would lift us one more plane above the animals. It was only later that I began to understand the urgency, the real *need* for it. If I'd felt that at first, well, I don't suppose I should ever have gone about things as I did. I should probably have tried to publish in the orthodox way—and, I think, have been suppressed. . . .

"As things were, I saw no great hurry. What was important was to build up a body of people, long-livers without their knowing it, but who would have a vested interest in fighting for it, and some influence, when the time should come."

She gave a little smile again.

"I know the way I did it can look funny. To your father I'm sure it's outrageous—like putting fizzy lemonade in the Holy Grail, or something—but I still can't think of any other way I could have managed it successfully. I've got them, you see. Almost a thousand women, nearly all of them either married to, or related to, people of influence. Once they understand the situation, I shall be extremely sorry for anyone who tries to legislate them out of their extra years of life."

"How did you do it?" Zephanie wanted to know.

"Once I had the idea, and turned it over, the better it seemed to look. I remember about someone who'd been caught smuggling pearls, and the way he'd done it was to hide the strings of real pearls in consignments of imitation pearls. . . .

"Well, after all, every woman's paper is littered with offers to 'preserve your youth,' 'keep those youthful contours,' and all the rest. Nobody really believes a word of it, of course, but it's a sort of sure-fire dream appeal, and people seem to have developed an unbreakable habit of hoping and trying. So, if I could show results, well, they'd be delighted, but at the same time they've been bitten so often they'd never really believe it was the genuine thing, not for years and years. They'd congratulate themselves on being more favored than others. They'd ascribe it to diet. They'd go so far as to concede that I must have something a bit better than my competitors had, perhaps. But actually *believe* that it was the genuine article, after thousands of years of phony recipes for youth! No, no, not they.

"I won't say I wasn't a bit shocked by the idea myself at first. But I told myself: 'This is the twentieth century, for what it's worth. It's not the age of reason, or even the nineteenth century, it's the era of flummery, and the day of the devious approach. Reason's gone into the backrooms where it works to devise means by which people can be induced to emote in the desired direction. And when I say people I mean women. To hell with reason. The thing is to jockey them some way or other into buying what you want them to buy. So it turned out I was pretty well in tune with modern salesmanship, really.

"Once I had decided it could be done, the first thing was to make sure of my resources. I had to be certain of a steady supply of what your father calls lichenin—which I called tertianin. So I announced that I was going on a round-the-world trip for a year.

"I did, too—though nearly all the time was actually spent in East Asia. First I went to Hong Kong, and made contact with your father's shipping agent there. He introduced me to a Mr. Craig. Mr. Craig had been a friend of the Mr. Macdonald who sent the shipments which had the Tertius lichen in them, but Mr. Macdonald himself had died nearly a year before. However, Mr. Craig put me on to several people who had worked with Mr. Macdonald, and eventually I met a Mr. McMurtie who had been on the expedition that found the first lot of lichens. So I engaged Mr. McMurtie, and he made arrangements, and got permits somehow from the Chinese.

"I expect your father told you that I put *Mongolensis* into the name I gave the first batch, but that turned out to be a misnomer. The stuff really comes from Hokiang which is a province of Manchuria, and lies north of Vladivostock. Fortunately, the permits came through in the spring, so were able to start off right away.

"Mr. McMurtie got us to the place without much difficulty, but it was very disappointing. There wasn't much of the *Tertius* there. It was practically restricted to a thousand acres or so where it grew in patches around a small lake. That was worse than I had thought. We found the man and his family who collect it and send it off, and when we'd talked to him it was pretty clear that if I arranged to have it collected from there, there soon wouldn't be any left. However, the man did not think this was the only lot, so we organized a search over quite an area around—nobody interfered; it's a kind of marshy moorland country with bits of very rough grazing. Altogether we discovered five more *Tertius* sites; three somewhat bigger than your father's source, two smaller, all within a radius of about twenty-five miles.

"That was better, but unless it also occurs somewhere else altogether, there's no doubt that the supply is quite limited. However, I was able to commission the locals for an annual collection of a standard quantity, and Mr. McMurtie made arrangements by which it is taken down to Dairen, and eventually shipped here via Nagasaki. I did my best to work out a quantity which would not deplete it, but the *Tertius* is so slow growing, and there can't be much margin. Unfortunately, there doesn't seem to be any reliable way of finding out just how it's holding up, short of going there to see. We can't hope to increase the supply much unless we find some other sites, or discover some other species which will also yield lichenin.

"In fact, I never did like the supply position at all. It's worked all right so far—presumably because nobody but us has ever been interested. But any trouble in those parts might cut it off entirely. What's more, not only is the stuff under Chinese control, but if the Russians were to hear of it and take an interest in it, well, it's in a sort of promontory of Manchuria, with the Russian frontier no more than two hundred miles away, in three directions....

"I tell you this because I think someone ought to know. I have a feeling that the thing cannot be kept quiet much longer, but when it does come out, the real source of the supplies is one thing that must not in any circumstances be made public. I'm sure your father appreciates that as much as I do, but I'd like you to mention it to him. I've laid my own red herring trail. In fact, I've got quite a flock of red herrings for defense in depth. I very much hope he has, too. As for yourself, you're only one of the subjects treated. If you are ever questioned; first, you don't know anything about any lichens; second, you haven't the least idea where it came from. It's vitally important that the source shouldn't be known; but it's just about as important that knowledge of it shouldn't be lost. I, or your father, or both of us, will be the chief targets, of course, and—you never can tell. It'll be a matter of life and death, you know."

"I'm beginning to understand," said Zephanie.

"Well, once that was fixed," Diana went on, "I came back here, and I went into business.—And," she added, looking round the room, and out at the little garden, "I've done pretty well at it. Why not?"

Zephanie did not respond. She remained sunk in thought, blankly staring at a painting on the wall. Then she turned and looked at Diana.

"I wish you'd not told me that—about the source of the lichen, I mean."

"If only you knew how often I've wished I'd never seen any lichen at all," said Diana.

"No, it's that I'm not to be trusted," Zephanie told her, and explained about Richard.

Diana considered her thoughtfully.

"You'd had a shock, of course, a considerable shock. I shouldn't think it's likely to happen a second time."

"No. I understand it better now. I was so muddled. It seemed as if I were all by myself then. Just me, trying to face it all alone. I was frightened, but now I know there are lots of us, it's different. All the same, there's no excuse—I did let it out."

"Did he believe it—or did he just think you were being silly?"

"I—I'm not sure. He must know there was something in it, I think."

Diana considered again.

"This young man, Richard. What sort of a young man? Brains or beef?"

"Both," said Zephanie.

"Fortunate young man. Do you trust him?"

"I'm going to marry him," Zephanie said sharply.

"That's no answer. Women are constantly marrying men they don't trust. What's his job?"

"He's a lawyer."

"He ought to have some idea of discretion then, at least. If you have confidence in him, take him down to see your father, and have it out. If you haven't, tell me now."

"I have," Zephanie told her.

"Very well. Then do that before he decides to start looking for the fire behind the smoke, on his own account."

"But—"

"But what? Either you've got to let him know more, or shut him up."

"Yes," agreed Zephanie meekly.

"Fine," said Diana, with an air of having settled that. "Now I want to know a bit more about you. What factor is your father using for you?"

"What what?"

"Factor. Is he increasing your time by three, four, five?"

"Oh, I see. He said three, both Paul and me."

"I see. Cautious—of course he would be with you two. I'll bet he's using a bigger factor himself."

"You mean it can be longer still? I didn't know that."

"I'm using five. It's safe, but more detectable. The Nefertiti clients are mostly on two, or two and a half, to three."

"But how on earth can you do it at all without their knowing?"

"Oh, it isn't difficult. There are so many things an expensive place does in the cause of beauty—and who can sort out which results in what? . . . And who cares, as long as the consequences are to the good?" Diana frowned.

"The only thing that has really caused me anxiety is these wretched women who won't tell us soon enough that they are going to have babies so that one can knock them off the lichenin injections in time to make little difference from normal. I'm always afraid that one day some of the doctors will put their heads together, and some busybody will produce a column of statistics showing that on an average it takes a Nefertiti client longer to have a baby than it takes anyone else. That could be awkward, and pretty difficult to explain away harmlessly. However, it hasn't happened *yet*. . . .

"In fact, we've managed wonderfully smoothly until we came up against this Mrs. Wilberry and her damned allergy. That was bad luck. Genuine enough, poor thing. She swelled up quite alarmingly: vivid rash all over; asthmatic congestion causing painful difficulty in breathing. There's no doubt she had a nasty time of it, but she'd have settled for a few hundreds, and have been glad to, if her lawyer hadn't worked on her. Ten thousand, he put her up to claiming! Ten thousand—on the strength of a mild recurrence of symptoms whenever she eats mushrooms. Would you believe it! And the man stuck like a mule at five thousand—which is going to be quite trying enough when the news gets round. Mushrooms, my God!"

Diana gloomed for some moments, but then threw the mood off.

"Perhaps we'll weather it yet," she said. "And if we don't— well, anyway, there can't be so much longer to run now. . . ."

7

Paul's secretary caught him as he was on the point of leaving the office.

"Dr. Saxover's on the telephone, sir."

Paul turned back and picked up the receiver.

"That you, Paul?" Francis's voice asked, without warmth.

"Yes, Father."

"I had a visit from your wife this morning, Paul. I think you might at least have had the courtesy to tell me you had informed her."

"I did tell you I must tell her, Father. I explained the position as I saw it. And that's the way I still see it."

"When did you tell her?"

"The next morning."

"Five days ago, eh? Did she say anything about coming to see me?"

"Well, yes, she did. But I wasn't sure if she meant it. We—er—well, we said some rather heated things at the time. Then when she didn't go down to Darr right away, I thought she might have changed her mind and decided to wait a bit."

"She didn't wait very long."

"What did she want?"

"Really, Paul! What do you think she wanted—demanded?"

"Did you—?"

"Yes, I did. I thought you'd better know."

There was a click as the receiver at the other end went down. Paul held his own instrument for some seconds and then put it back on the rest, slowly.

Jane was not in when he got home. It was past nine o'clock when she arrived. She went straight to the bedroom, and presently there was the sound of bathwater running. Half an hour later she came into the sitting-room clad in a quilted white dressing-gown. Paul, his third whisky beside him, looked at her with an unamiable expression that she did not bother to notice.

"I've been down to Darr," she said, with an air of getting it in first.

"So I've heard. Why didn't you tell me you were going?"

"I did."

"You didn't tell me when."

"Would it have made any difference?"

"There are ways and ways of doing things. I could have warned him to expect you."

"I didn't want him warned. Why should he have time to think up more reasons for keeping me out of it—leaving me with a short life while the rest of you have long ones? I knew what I meant to get, and I got it."

"So I gathered. He was pretty terse about it on the telephone."

"I don't suppose he liked it. How do you suppose I've liked his deliberately excluding me?"

"It wasn't deliberate—not in the way you mean. Won't you understand that he's got to be careful? He's got to take every precaution against it leaking out. He's thinking of the disorganization that will follow any hint of it. The responsibility—why look at me like that? This isn't funny, Jane. It's very far from funny."

"I think it is rather. Naïveté is, you know, and a little touching.

Bless the boy, I think you really do believe anything your eminent father tells you, don't you? Isn't it about time you grew up a bit, my pet?—or does this stuff affect the mind, and keep that young, too?"

Paul stared at her.

"What on earth are you talking about?"

"Your father, my dear—and his responsibility, and his conscience, and his duty to humanity. Would it surprise you to know that your distinguished father is also an accomplished hypocrite?"

"Really, Jane, I won't—"

"Yes. I see it really does."

"Jane. I am not going to—"

But Jane took no notice of his interruption. She went on:

"You just took in all you were told, didn't you? It didn't even occur to you to inquire who this Diana Brackley is, and what she's doing."

"I know what she's doing. She runs Nefertiti Ltd."

Jane looked disconcerted for a moment.

"You never told me that."

"Why should I?"

She gazed at him hard.

"I really think your father must have you hypnotized, or something. You *knew* that—and yet you never realized that she's been acting as the outlet for this stuff for years. Oh, she doesn't put it across as an antigerone. She simply runs an uncannily successful beauty business. She charges what she likes for her treatments—and gets it. *That's* what's really been happening to the secret which is too dangerous to make public. And a very nice thing they must have been making out of it between them, for years."

Paul went on staring at her.

"I don't believe it."

"Then why didn't he deny it?"

"He did to Zephanie. She asked if Diana was his agent. He denied it flatly."

"He didn't to me."

"What did he say?"

"He didn't say anything much. It wouldn't have been any good his denying it, anyway. Not once I'd found out."

"Yes, I'm beginning to understand why he might think that," Paul said slowly. "What did he do?"

"He did as I asked." She put her right hand reminiscently on her left upper arm. "He couldn't very well refuse, could he?"

Paul went on looking at her, thinking.

"I'd better ring him up," he said.

"Why?" she asked sharply. "He'll just confirm what I told you."

Paul said: "I told you about this in confidence because I thought that as my wife you had a right to know about it as soon as I did. You knew I'd not leave it at that. You knew I'd see that he gave you this antigerone stuff in due course. Why on earth couldn't you wait a few days longer instead of resorting to black-mail?"

"Blackmail! Really, Paul—"

"That's what it was. You know it was. Now God knows what speculations your inquiries about Diana may have stirred up."

"I'm not altogether a fool, Paul."

"But you've made inquiries of someone, and your married name does happen to be Saxover. I'd better ring Darr."

"I've told you what happened. He was cold, barely polite—but he did it."

"You mean you *think* he did it. What I want to know is just what he *did* do."

"What do you mean?" she said uneasily.

"Well, if someone came to me making demands with threats I'm not at all sure I should do exactly as she asked—particularly if I knew that she could have no real way of checking for some time. It would be easy to substitute—"

He broke off suddenly, disconcerted by the way she was staring at him, noticing that she had gone pale.

"It's all right," he said. "It wouldn't be anything harmful."

"How—how do I know?" she said. "If he'd play a trick like that— But he didn't have time. He didn't know I was coming," she added, uncertainly.

Paul got up.

"At least we can tell whether it *looks* like the right kind of implant," he said. "Let me see the incision."

"No!" she exclaimed, and in a tone that startled him. He frowned.

"What's the matter?" he said. "Don't you want to know whether he gave you the right stuff or not?"

He reached a hand toward her. She pulled back into her chair.

"No!" she repeated. "Of course it's all right. Get away from me! Leave me alone!"

Paul paused, looking down on her curiously.

"This isn't making sense," he said slowly. "What are you afraid of?"

"Afraid of? What do you mean?" He still stood looking at her. She said: "I'm sick of this. I told you what happened, and I'm tired. Please get out of the way. I want to go to bed."

But Paul moved a short step closer.

"Have you been lying about this, Jane? Wasn't there an implantation at all?"

"Of course there was."

"Then I'd like to see."

She shook her head.

"Not now, I'm tired out."

Paul's irritation got the better of him. He made a quick snatch and pulled the dressing-gown sleeve down over her left shoulder, far enough to show a neat white bandage round her upper arm. Paul looked at it.

"I see," he said.

"It's a pity you can't take my word for it," she said coldly.

He shook his head slowly.

"You aren't making it easy to take your word," he told her. "I know very well how my father dresses the wound afterward. That's not his way of doing it."

"No," she agreed. "The blood soaked through. I had to put on a new one."

"And you managed that neat dressing single-handed? How clever of you." He paused, and then went on in a voice that had hardened. "Now, I've had about enough of this. What else have you been up to? What is it you're trying to hide?"

Jane attempted to recapture her earlier manner, but it was a poor imitation. She'd never known him to look at her with the expression he wore now, and her confidence in her ability to manage him was wilting.

"Hide?" she repeated, unconvincingly. "I don't know what you mean. I've just told you . . ."

"You've just told me that you held up my father with threats. What I want to know is what else you've been up to—and I intend to find out. . . ." Paul told her.

—

Up on the fifth floor of the deliberately unostentatious building off Curzon Street where Nefertiti Ltd carried out its mission the communicator on Diana's desk gave a subdued buzz. She flipped a switch. The attenuated voice of her secretary said:

"I have a Miss Brendon here from the second floor, Miss Brackley. She's very anxious to see you. I have told her that the proper approach is through Miss Rollridge but she still insists that she must see you herself, on a personal matter. She has been up here twice already today."

"She's with you now, Sarah?"

"Yes, Miss Brackley."

Diana considered. She decided that even a third approach would not have got past Sarah Tallwyn unless there was a good reason.

"Very well, then, Sarah. I'll see her."

Miss Brendon was ushered in. She turned out to be a small, pretty, golden-haired girl; somewhat doll-like until you noticed the set of her chin, the line of her mouth, and the still-lingering light of battle in her blue eyes. Diana studied her, and she, with almost equal candor, studied Diana.

"Why didn't you put it through Miss Rollridge?" Diana inquired.

"I would have done, if it had been an administrative matter," the girl told her. "But you are my employer, and I thought you ought to know. Besides . . ."

"Besides—what?"

"Well, I thought it might be better if other people didn't know."

"Even the director of your department?"

Miss Brendon hesitated.

"People talk such a lot in this place," she said.

Diana nodded slowly.

"Well now, what is it?" she asked.

The girl said:

"I went to a party last night, Miss Brackley. Just a meal and dancing in a kind of club. There were six of us. The only one I knew was the man who invited me. While we were eating, they started talking about Mrs. Wilberry. One of the men said he was interested in allergies, and wondered what could have caused hers. My friend who'd taken me said I worked at Nefertiti, so I ought to know. Of course, I said I didn't, because I don't. But this other man kept on talking about it, and kind of slipping in questions now and then. After a bit I began to have a feeling that the whole thing about Mrs. Wilberry hadn't come up by accident—I couldn't say quite why. Well, this other man was very attentive to me during the evening, and in the end he invited me to come out with him tonight. I didn't much want to, so I said I couldn't. He suggested tomorrow night. So I said I'd let him know, thinking it would be easier to refuse over the telephone." She paused. "I suppose I look a bit green, but I'm not really. I wondered why he was turning on the charm, and I thought over the questions he'd been asking about Nefertiti. So I made some inquiries about him, and found out that he is a journalist, quite a well-known one, I think, called Marlin. He works for the *Sunday Prole.*"

Diana nodded thoughtfully, her eyes on the girl's face.

"I agree that you're not green, Miss Brendon. I take it you've not mentioned it to *anyone* else here?" she asked.

"No, Miss Brackley."

"Good. Well now, I think the best thing—if you've no objection—is for you to meet this Mr. Marlin tomorrow evening, and tell him the sort of thing he wants to know."

"But I don't know what—"

"That's all right. I'll get Miss Tallwyn to brief you."

Miss Brendon looked puzzled. Diana said:

"You've not been in this trade long, have you, Miss Brendon?"

"Less than a year, Miss Brackley."

"And before that?"

"I was training as a nurse, but then my father died. My mother had very little money, so I had to find something that would bring in more."

"I see. . . . When you get to know the trade better, Miss Brendon, you will find it quite fascinating. Nobody actually cuts throats, but about ninety-five percent of us would fill life-jackets with lead, or sell our grandmothers to South America if there were any profit in it. Now, if you don't talk to this Mr. Marlin, the poor man is going to be put to all the trouble of contriving a contact with some other member of our staff.

"I much prefer to know what he is being told. Besides, if he is a careful man you won't be his only contact. He'll want to check. So we must do our best to see that things tally for him. Now, how, I wonder, can we steer him unobtrusively on to a second contact?"

Miss Brendon's formal manner relaxed as they discussed tactics. By the end of the interview she was enjoying herself.

"All right then," Diana concluded. "Have a good evening. Remember that in our calling we make the most of our opportunities; we never choose one of the modestly priced dishes. That would be almost suspiciously out of character; besides, the more exotic ones will show him he's not going to get his information cheaply, so he'll have more confidence in it when he does get it. When he makes you an offer, put your price at double, then compromise at about fifty percent above what he originally offered. It's a sort of convention which helps to reassure them."

"I see," said Miss Brandon, "and what shall I do with the money, Miss Brackley?"

"God bless the girl! You do what you like with it, Miss Brendon. You'll have earned it. Now off with you. Call in on Miss Tallwyn when the shop shuts, and she'll brief you. Let me know how it goes."

After she had left, Diana pressed the communicator switch.

"Oh, Sarah. Bring me the file on Miss Brandon, will you?"

Sarah Tallwyn duly appeared, bearing a slender folder.

"Nice girl. . . . Nice change," Diana commented.

"Capable," agreed Miss Tallwyn. "The sort that might have made a good matron one day. Pity she had to come to this."

"Dear Sarah. So tactful," said Diana, turning the cover of the file.

———

"Is that all?" inquired Richard.

He looked down at the bandage on his left arm, and fingered it gently.

"Quite undramatic, I'm afraid. The films do this sort of thing much better," Francis told him. He went on: "This will dissolve very slowly, and be absorbed into the system. One could use injections, in fact I did use them myself at first, but it's a nuisance— and less satisfactory, too. It gives a series of jolts, whereas this is smooth and steady."

Richard glanced at the bandage again.

"It's still difficult to believe. I don't really know what to say, sir."

"Don't try. Put it on the practical level—once I knew that you knew about it, it became a matter of sheer expediency to offer you the benefits. Besides, Zephanie would have insisted before long, anyway. What *is* important is that you should keep it *entirely* to yourself."

"I will. But—" he hesitated, and went on, "aren't you taking a bit of a risk, sir? I mean, we've met three or four times, but, well, you don't know a great deal about me."

"You'd be surprised, my dear fellow. At Darr," he explained, "we have always several projects on hand, some of them of great potential value. Naturally, our competitors are interested in finding out what they can about us. A few of them are none too scrupulous. They would not hesitate to use any means to their end. When one has an attractive daughter it therefore becomes one's distasteful duty to learn something about her friends, and their backgrounds and connections. When they turn out to be employed by subsidiaries of large-scale manufacturing chemists, or to have uncles on the board of chemical concerns, a broad hint is usually enough to send them on their way." He paused thoughtfully. "Incidentally, I should take particular care not to let Mr. Farrier get any inkling of this."

Richard looked at him in surprise.

"Tom Farrier, but he's an advertising man. I knew him at school."

"I daresay, but you've only fairly recently come across him again, and introduced him to Zephanie, haven't you? Did you know that his mother remarried three or four years ago, and her husband happens to be the head research man with Chemicultures Limited? No, I see you didn't. Ah, well, it's a devious world, my boy.

"Let's go downstairs again. By the way, I don't think we'll mention any of this to Zephanie. It is, as I said, a distasteful precaution, but necessary."

"Hullo, Richard," Zephanie said, as they entered the sitting-room. "Itches, doesn't it? That soon goes, though. Then you wouldn't know anything has happened."

"I hope not," Richard told her, doubtfully. "My first depressing thought was that since one of my days is going to equal three of anyone else's, I might have to cut down to one meal a day. I still don't see why not."

"Because unless you go torpid, or hibernate, or something, your physical structure is still going to need the same quantity of calories to fuel it and sustain it," Zephanie said, with an air of pointing out the obvious.

"But—oh, well, I'll take your word for that," Richard conceded. "I might as well. I'm finding it hard enough to have faith in any of it. In fact, but for the name Saxover on the packet. . . ." He shrugged, frowned, and went on: "You must forgive me, Dr. Saxover, but what I still find hardest to take is the—the secret recipe—er—set-up, if you'll forgive me. You've both explained most patiently to me, I know. It'll sink in, perhaps, later on, but, as yet, I can't get rid of a feeling of anachronism—rather as if I'd suddenly fallen among alchemists. I hope I don't sound offensive, I don't mean to be. It's just that this is the twentieth century, and science doesn't—at least I didn't think it did—behave like this any more; not as if it were afraid of being taken up for witchcraft, I mean." He ended by looking at them both a little uncertainly.

"It doesn't like behaving in this way, I assure you," Francis replied. "And *if* there were adequate supplies, or *if* we could make the synthesis, it would not have to. That is the crux of the whole situation. Well, now, if you'll excuse me, there are some things I must see to before dinner," he told them, and took himself off.

"I suppose," Richard said as the door closed, "I suppose I shall really begin to believe in this one day—up till now I've got stuck at the stage of accepting it as an intellectual proposition."

"I suppose so, too," Zephanie said, "but it isn't easy. In fact it's a lot more difficult than I thought. It means pulling to pieces the whole basic pattern we accepted in childhood. The ground plan—young children, middle-aged parents, elderly grandparents, the whole idea of the generations rolling on like that is so fundamental. There's such a lot we shall just have to scrap. So many yardsticks and reference-points that won't be any good any more."

She turned to look at him earnestly.

"Ten days ago I was happy at the thought of spending fifty years with you, Richard—if we should be lucky. Of course, that wasn't how I put it to myself—I just thought of spending my life with you. Now, I just don't know . . . Can one spend a hundred and fifty years—two hundred years, perhaps—with somebody? *Can* two people go on loving one another that long? What happens? How much does one change in all that time? We can't know. There's no one who can tell us."

Richard moved beside her, and put his arm round her.

"Darling. Nobody can cross all the bridges in even fifty years, before he reaches them. And couldn't it be that some of the rough patches are there just because there usually is no more than fifty years? We can't tell that, either. Of course we shall have to plan differently, but it's no good worrying about that a hundred years ahead. As for the rest, is it so very different, really? We couldn't *know* our future ten days ago; we still can't *know* it now— only that we shall probably have more of it than we expected. So why not start off just as we should have done—for better, or for worse? That's what I still want to do, don't you?"

"Oh, yes, Richard, yes. It's only—"

"Only what?"

"I don't quite know . . . The loss of the shape, the pattern . . . Being a grandmother, perhaps, when one's only the equivalent of twenty-seven, or a great-grandmother aged thirty-five. Still being able to have a baby oneself after ninety years or so. And that's only with a factor of three. It'll all be such a queer mess . . . I don't think I want it—but I don't not want it, either. . . ."

"Darling, you're talking as if all normal-length lives were planned. They aren't, you know. People have to learn how to live them—and by the time they find out, they're nearly gone. No time to remedy the mistakes. We shall have time to learn how to live, and then time to enjoy living. It's still not real to me, but I can see how your Diana could be right. More time is important. If we live longer we shall learn more about living, about how to live. We shall understand more. It will be a fuller, richer life. It *must* be. No one could fill two hundred years with the trivialities that are good enough for fifty years . . .

"Come on now, darling. It isn't to be worried about. It's to be *lived.* It's going to be an adventure. Make up your mind to that. We're going to *enjoy* finding out about it together. Come now— aren't we?"

Zephanie turned her face up to his. She let the troubled look clear, and smiled.

"Oh, yes, Richard, darling. We are . . . of course we are. . . ."

8

Dominating the sparse Monday-morning post beside Francis Saxover's breakfast plate was a slightly bulging envelope addressed to him in a dashing hand which he failed to recognize. He opened it to find that though most of the content was newspaper, there was also a brief covering letter:

Dear Francis,

Recalling that on Sundays at Darr one customarily exercises only in the well-tended acres of the Observer and/or Times, I suspect that the enclosed may not have reached your attention, and feel that you should be acquainted with their contents.

The explanation is that one of the red herrings in my defence system has now taken wing, and is likely, I think, to prove a credit to its stable. The situation is made still happier by the apparent fact that the left hand of Fleet Street did not know what the right hand was doing, and that A is probably very hopping mad with B.

Yours, in haste,
Diana Brackley

Puzzled, Francis picked up the folded piece of newspaper marked A. It revealed itself as a complete page from the *Sunday Radar,* with certain parts marked by red crosses, the whole being headed by four pairs of photographs, and the announcement:

CORNER IN BEAUTY BROKEN FOR
RADAR READERS

Beneath, he read:

Great news for YOU, YOU, AND YOU!

They'll tell you that money can't buy everything. There are things like the sun in the morning and the moon at night, great big smiles, loving hearts, and a flock of other things that don't carry cash tags, and they could be right at that. But you know and I know that the way we've got things arranged in this modern world money can still help to give you a much smoother ride through life—may even run to a gold-plated Daimler if you're lucky.

Now take a look at the gallery of beauty above, and see what I mean. In each case, the upper picture is the way she looked ten years ago, and the lower is the way she looks today. Now, compare the picture *you* had taken ten years ago with what looks out of your mirror. See? A lot more difference than there is on the comparisons on this page, isn't there?

And what does it cost a socialite to have ten years go past and scarcely leave a mark? Well, our gallery of ladies reckon that £300 to £400 a year, or could be more, paid to a high-toned beauty establishment in London's Mayfair to achieve it is money well spent.

And maybe that's so—*if* you have that kind of money, and don't mind handing it out.

Most of our readers, though, will be wistfully telling themselves they'd have to win a treble chance to afford it. But no. This time they are wrong. Now, thanks to the *Radar* everyone, but everyone, *can* afford it.

The article went on to explain that *Radar* investigators had uncovered the secret of preserving beauty used in this establishment, and that far from costing three hundred pounds a year, it could easily be covered by three hundred pence. It proposed to share this discovery with its readers.

A series of exclusive articles commencing in next week's *Sunday Radar* will reveal the whole secret, telling every woman reader all she needs to know about preserving her youth, as is her right.

So make certain to place an order for next week's *Sunday Radar*—the paper that finds out what YOU want to know!

Francis, with a feeling of having been given the minimum amount of information grudgingly, laid the sheet aside wondering how many weekly articles the *Radar* would be able to shell off before it arrived at the kernel. From his point of view, however, the interest lay in the red line which encircled the photographs, and then added: "Clients!"

He then picked up the other cutting, a more modest affair in the form of a double-column panel from the *Sunday Prole*. It, too, was headed with pairs of contrasted photographs, though this time only two pairs, and in smaller format. Nor were the ladies whose past and present appearances were compared here members of the quartet that appeared in the *Radar*. The heading this time was:

AGE SHALL NOT . . . !

and the by-line, Gerald Marlin. His piece began:

It has been no secret around Mayfair this week that a certain beauty establishment whose name is a household word— provided it is an upper-income bracket, high expense-account household—settled for damages on a lavish scale rather than expose its workings to vulgar notice in the law-courts—and rather, perhaps, than have to answer pertinent questions in public. So silken skirts have been drawn aside from contamination, and privacy, it may even be virtue, preserved, at a price.

An allergy is a whimsical thing, given to revealing itself unexpectedly, and, sometimes, distressingly. One's sympathy must go out to a lady who not only had to suffer great discomfort, but had to suffer it alone, without the support of a husband whose important South American interests caused him to depart thither somewhat hurriedly a year ago, and kept him from being at her bedside during the critical time—or, indeed, from returning at all. And as well as our sympathy, she deserves our congratulations. She hasn't done at all badly out of it.

But an allergy does not always distress the afflicted alone: the provider of its cause may also be far from happy about it, particularly if the provider is a firm of standing with a reputation for helping wealthy ladies to cheat the years, which, as our pictures above eloquently testify, is by no means ill-deserved. Accidents will, of course, happen, but it is preferred by elegant establishments that their happening there should be known to as few people as possible. For one thing, it is better not to perturb valued and valuable clients; for another, all trades have their secrets, and it can be worth agreeing to generous compensation if one thereby avoids having to admit in public that the source of one's not inconsiderable profit is not an exotic product of Arabia, or a subtle substance from Circassia but a simple something which can be acquired far nearer home, for merely the cost of its collection and carriage.

Francis Saxover, growing a little tired of Mr. Marlin's turgid style of innuendo, skipped until he came to the last paragraph:

The source of the sensitive client's discomfort, and what precautions she should take against its recurrence, remain, in spite of the otherwise highly satisfactory terms of the settlement, unknown even to herself. It seems unjust that the lady should be left in such a state of anxiety, never knowing from moment to moment when she may encounter a substance that will cause a discomfort which might well be quite unprofitable on its second manifestation. So, out of sympathy with her plight, may we offer her the following advice: let her avoid, if possible, the shores of Galway Bay: but if she must go to Galway Bay, let her avoid bathing there; however, if there are circumstances which make it impossible for her to avoid bathing in Galway Bay, she should at all costs avoid coming into contact with a certain type of seaweed to be found there. Provided she takes this simple precaution she should be able to enjoy her generous compensation with an easy mind—unless, of course, it should happen that other cosmeticians are tempted to make their fortunes out of a magic weed which has proved itself worth a great deal more than its weight in gold.

After he had finished breakfast, Francis broke his usual habit of going straight up to his laboratory, and made his way, instead, to his study. There, with his hand on the telephone, he hesitated which number to call, and decided that Diana was unlikely to have left her flat yet. It was the right choice.

"Thank you for the newspaper cuttings, Diana," he said. "Just as long as it did not occur to anyone to wonder why Mrs. Wilberry should be allergic to mushrooms as a result of treatment with seaweed, it might have worked well."

"Pouf!" said Diana. "Nobody's going to. Allergies are far too erratic and mysterious in their ways for anyone to be surprised. And I take exception to 'might.' It's working like a bomb. All my hated rivals spent all yesterday on the telephone madly trying to find out more. Mr. Marlin must have been offered fortunes for details. Almost every woman's paper already has a representative waiting for me at the office; and the girl on the switchboard says we ought to employ a parrot to say 'No comment' to all the newspapers and free-lancers who are ringing up. I understand there is an inquiry from the Ministry of Agriculture and Fisheries with regard to any permits issued to me by the Board of Trade to import seaweed from the Irish Republic."

"That's interesting," Francis said. "They can't have had time to act on what was in Sunday's papers. They must have got it from somewhere else."

"Certainly," agreed Diana. "I know where Marlin got it from, but a week ago I made sure that it reached three of my least discreet girls in strictest confidence. It could have got anywhere by now. There's going to be no end of fun over this."

"Look here," Francis said. "I regret having to strike a sour note at this stage, but I fear I must. I don't think I'd better tell you now, but I'm coming up to London today, and I think we ought to discuss it. Can you dine with me? What about Claridge's at eight-thirty? Would that suit?"

"The time would, but not the place. It's even more important now that your name shouldn't be linked with mine. And I'm going to be a marked woman while this is on, so you can't come here. I suggest we make it a little place called The Atomium in Charlotte Street. Nobody's likely to see us there."

"It seems improbable," agreed Francis. "Very well. The Atomium, at eight-thirty."

"Good," she said. "I'm looking forward to seeing you again after all this time, Francis. And I do so want to talk to you, and explain things more." She paused, and then added: "You sounded . . . Is it very serious, Francis?"

"Yes. I'm afraid it is," he told her.

—

"Oh, it's you, is it?" said the editor. "You're looking very pleased with yourself."

"I am, rather," Gerald Marlin told him.

"A good thing, perhaps, because I don't know that I am—with you, I mean. I've had Wilkes from the *Radar* breathing noxious death-wishes down my telephone. You've queered a whole campaign he had cooked up."

"Too bad—too bad," Gerald said, cheerfully.

"What happened?"

"Well, as I told you, at the rate they paid the Willerby woman there was clearly something that Nefertiti didn't want publicly known—and I'm not surprised. It's a shattering thought, but that outfit really does seem to do something pretty remarkable for its clients. Anyway I contrived a contact there, an innocent-looking maiden who adores caviare and champagne, and haggles like a horse-dealer. I decided Quaglino's would be about right, and as we were going in, I saw a young woman who was sitting in the lounge look at my contact with a startled expression, and then pretend not to have seen her. My contact looked a bit taken aback, too, so I asked what the trouble was. She was just explaining that the other girl was also from Nefertiti's when a man went up to her and greeted her—Freddy Rammer, from the *Radar,* if you please. I turned away so that he'd not spot me, and when they'd safely gone into the restaurant we decided to dine elsewhere.

"Well, I got it on the grapevine that the *Radar* was planning a be-your-own-beauty-queen series, and put two and two together. It was a bit of a blow. I mean, it would have been nice to hang on awhile, and see whether one couldn't do something about acquiring seaweed rights in Galway Bay. But, obviously it couldn't wait for that, so I wired a friend in Dublin to get a head start by making inquiries about legal rights over seaweed, in Irish law."

The editor shook his head.

"You'd probably have to petition the Pope, or something," he said. "It's likely to be a pretty serious matter with the Irish. They eat the stuff."

"They *what?*"

"Eat it. They call it dulse."

Gerald shook his head in his turn, though whether in doubt, or out of sympathy for the Irish, was not clear.

"Anyway," he went on, "it was really too late. I had either to let the *Radar* scoop us, or spike their little game. My unfortunate friend over there has probably been trampled to death by now. I shan't be the only one who thought of getting in early to stake a claim. Begorra, 'tis a fine sight Dublin must be this morning with all the covered wagons streaming out of the city, lashing their lathered teams westwards across the rolling bogs."

"What the devil do you think you're talking about?" the editor demanded.

"Gold rush, old boy." He sang gently to himself.

"Oh, there's lot of gold so I've been told
On the bank of the Galway Bay—oh!"

"Mind you," he went on, "I'm not without a stake in several of the prospecting parties. Just about every beauty-dope maker in the kingdom—with the pointed exception of Nefertiti—rang me up yesterday, wanting to know more. I did my best to secure a participating interest, but I'm afraid it's pretty chancey. The thing that's held me back from a fortune," he confided, "is that there must be dozens of kinds of seaweed on the Galway strands, and frankly, I haven't a clue on which is the magical kind. And that unfortunately is a bit vital. It really means that if the *Radar* has identified the kind, they can still pull one over us."

The editor of the *Sunday Prole* thought for a moment, and shook his head.

"No. Wilkes wouldn't have blown off as he did . . . but he

might, though. He may think we've identified it, too, and are keeping it up our sleeves. In any case we'd better try. The thing to do is to find out where the stuff is processed, and liberate a specimen of it. Worth trying. Could do a lot for the female readership. . . ."

—

Diana moved aside the fat red candle which stood between them. By its light they studied one another. At last Francis said, in a curious tone:

"How strange that knowing should be different from seeing."

Diana went on looking without speaking. She became aware that her hand on the table was trembling, and hid it from sight. Her eyes went over his face, feature by feature, slowly. With an effort she asked:

"How angry are you with me—Francis?"

He shook his head.

"I'm not angry. I was. When I first knew, I was very angry indeed—until I began to understand why. When I had sorted it out into shock, hurt vanity, and alarm—mostly alarm, I knew it wouldn't do any good to hide myself behind anger. I had to look at myself; I found that fourteen years had taken away my right to be angry—though not my right to be alarmed. That, I still am."

He paused, examining her face as closely as she had his. "Now," he went on, "now I am ashamed of being angry. I am ashamed of myself. My God! To have grudged it to you; to have wished that I had been able to prevent it! That's going to be a stain on my mind forever. Indelible, and unforgivable. No, I'm not angry, I'm humbled. But not only—"

He broke off at a touch on his arm. "What is it?"

The waiter presented a menu.

"Oh, later on," he said irritably. "Bring us some sherry—dry. What was I saying?" he turned back to Diana.

Diana could not help him. She had taken in barely a word of

what he had already said. They went on looking at one another. Presently:

"You're not married?" he asked.

"No," said Diana.

He looked at her, puzzled. "I should have thought—" he began, and then broke off.

"What would you have thought?"

"I'm not quite sure—I—I suppose . . . *this* makes a difference?"

"To the extent that I don't have quite that awareness that most women seem to have of time pressing on their heels. But then I'm not much of a criterion: I've only known one man that I really wanted to marry," she said, and then, with an air of breaking away from the personal, went on: "I've been wondering, as a matter of fact, how marriage is going to mesh with the new order. One feels that people who can go on loving one another for two or three hundred years are probably pretty scarce."

"It doesn't mesh, as you put it, any too well with the present order," Francis remarked, "but it gets adapted. I don't see why it should not be adapted further. Fixed-term marriages, with options, as in leases, perhaps?"

Diana shook her head.

"It goes deeper than that. To be anthropological about it: the present primary social role of western woman is as wife; her secondary status is as mother; in upper and middle classes her tertiary status is sometimes that of companion—in other classes companionship can come a long way down the list, and in most non-western nations it scarcely rates at all. But with the prospect of an association extended from fifty to a possible two or three hundred years, a change is likely. It seems to me almost certain that companionship must move up to the primary status. And since our social pressures, popular propaganda, and quite a part of our trade, are now devoted to obtaining wife-status for our girls, a switch over to companion-status as the primary objective is going to cause one hell of a social revolution.

"Fortunately, that will only become apparent after a time, or we should have nearly all the young women tooth-and-nail against us. Wife-status is so easy; nature does most of it for you. You don't need brains, only appearance, and you can buy plenty of aids to that. But companion-status is a great deal more subtle; you have to use your loaf a bit, and you can't buy help in tubes and jars. That wouldn't be at all popular if it were perceived—but it won't be. They simply wouldn't believe it if it were explained to them. Everybody's prone to regard his local anthropological set-up as a law of nature. So we shall have all the dear little featherheads, and all the uxorious, and all the lazy-minded on our side, because the only thing they'll see in a longer life is lots and lots more time for lots and lots more bedroom games."

Watching her, Francis smiled slowly.

"That's authentic," he said. "Diana, my dear, there are things I had almost forgotten about you."

Diana became quite still.

"There's nothing—" she began, and then stopped. She blinked rapidly several times. "I—" she began again. Then abruptly she got up.

"I'll be back in a minute," she said, all in a rush, and was half-way across the restaurant by the time Francis could collect his wits.

He sat sipping his sherry and looking unseeingly at the wrap spread over the back of her empty chair. The waiter returned to slide a large menu before him, and another beside Diana's plate. Francis ordered more sherry. After ten minutes or so, Diana returned.

"We'd better choose," he said.

The waiter scribbled on his pad, and went away. There was an interval of silence which threatened to grow longer. Diana turned the red candle so that the wax should gutter down the other side. Then she said, a little briskly:

"Did you hear the six o'clock news?"

Francis had not.

"Then, for your information, the Ministry of Agriculture of the Republic of Ireland has published an order forbidding the export of seaweed except under license." She paused. "So 'tis after exporting the seaweed you've been Paddy?—Indayd, I have not!—Have you not now? Well, the governmint says you're not to do it any more without a piece of paper—Licenses," she added, "will presumably be issued when it has been decided what is the highest rate of duty this trade can possibly bear. There ought to be a lot of entertainment in it for everyone."

"Except perhaps the unfortunate women who've been put all agog to expect miracles of it," suggested Francis.

"Oh, they won't be much surprised," Diana assured him. "Miracle is a favorite word in women's papers. Nobody seriously expects it to *mean* anything. It's just a kind of dressing of manure to keep hope flourishing."

"Just what do you expect this seaweed nonsense to do?" he inquired.

"Provide a diversion," Diana told him. "My competitors are a fairly credulous lot. It'll take quite a time before they become really convinced that there's nothing in it. In the meantime customers will be clamoring for seaweed cream, seaweed lotion, seaweed breakfast food, and so on, so they'll do all right. I have a number of booster articles ready for placing here and there. There's one which reveals that beauty from seaweed is really a very ancient piece of knowledge now rediscovered—in fact the conception of Venus rising from the sea is really symbolic of this use of seaweed in primitive Greece. Nice, don't you think? I reckon that at the very minimum it should hold for two years, possibly twice that, before somebody perceives that it isn't getting the results that Nefertiti gets. By that time, it will be discovered that Nefertiti is now using an entirely new electronic device which, by ultra-sonic stimulation of the cell layers below the epidermis, restores that youthful resilience of tissues which is the secret of true *deep-seated* beauty. Oh, I can keep that sort of thing up for ages, if necessary. You needn't fear that the true source will come out for a long time yet."

Francis shook his head slowly.

"Ingenious," he admitted. "But I'm very much afraid it's all wasted, Diana."

"Oh, no!" she exclaimed, suddenly concerned at his tone. "Francis, what's happened?"

Francis looked round the room again. He did not recognize any of the other diners. They had no immediate neighbors, and there was enough general sound in the room to cover ordinary conversation in their corner. He said:

"That's what I wanted to tell you about. It isn't pleasant to have to admit, but in the circumstances, it could possibly be dangerous for you if I were not frank. It involves my daughter-in-law."

"I see. Zephanie told me about her. You mean Paul did decide to tell her?"

"Yes," Francis nodded. "He considered it his duty to tell her. He told her the next day. It was not, I gather, an entirely amicable occasion. They were both a little rattled—with the unfortunate result that he can't recall just how much he told her. But he did mention lichenin, and he did mention you."

Diana's fingers clenched.

"That," she said, with restraint, "would scarcely seem to be necessary."

"Oh, the whole damned thing was unnecessary. But apparently once he'd begun, he felt he had to account for my decision to tell him and Zephanie about it."

Diana nodded. "And what happened then?"

"Jane did not take it at all well. She brooded over it for several days, and seems to have made some inquiries for her own satisfaction. Then she came down to Darr to see me." He gave her an account of Jane's visit.

Diana frowned. "In other words, she staged a hold-up. Not a very nice young woman."

"Well," Francis said fairly, "she did have a point in considering that as my son's wife she had been unjustly excluded from a benefit that she should have been offered, but her approach was—er—far from tactful."

"But you did it for her? You gave her the lichenin?"

Francis nodded. "It would have been easy enough to fob her off for the time being with something else," he admitted. "But there seemed to be little to gain by that. I should have had to confess to it later on, or she would have discovered for herself; either would simply have made relations worse. The serious damage, I thought, had been done already—the fact that she knew about it at all. So I gave it to her. I gather you use injection, but I implanted, in soluble tablet form, as I do with Paul and Zephanie. I wish to God now that I'd had the sense to make it an injection."

"I don't see how that would have made any difference."

"It would. When she got home she told Paul she had been to see me—I suppose she thought it best; he'd be bound to inquire about the dressing on her arm. Paul guessed what sort of a line she would have taken with me, and was extremely angry about it. When he did see the dressing he knew at a glance that it was not done my way. He'd already got suspicious—something in her manner, I suppose. He insisted on examining the incision . . . and, well—the lichenin implant was not there.

"Jane went on obstinately protesting that it must have come out when she was putting on the new dressing. Sheer nonsense, of course—the incision had been opened, the tablet extracted, and the incision closed again, with a couple of stitches, as it had been before.

"But she stuck to her story, rubbish though it was. Finally she rushed off to the bedroom, and locked herself in. Paul spent the night in the spare room. When he woke up in the morning she had already gone—with two suitcases. . . . Nobody's seen her since."

Diana thought for some seconds.

"There really is no chance that it could have been an accident?" she asked.

"None whatever. The two stitches must have been removed and replaced. It would have been more intelligent to have inserted a harmless, similar-shaped tablet as a precaution. She might possibly have carried that off."

"But the implication is that she got it from you in order to take it to someone else?"

"Clearly. Probably with a promise that she would be treated again, once they had the secret of it."

"And a whacking good payment down, by the sound of her. How much could they learn from the tablet?"

"A lot less than they think, I imagine. Neither you nor I has been able to synthesize it in all this time. But we'd better assume she's told them all she knows. It will give them at least a line to work on."

"Does she know where it comes from?"

"No. Fortunately, I didn't tell Paul that."

"What do you suppose'll be their next step?"

"Look into our imports, and try to trace something from those, I should imagine."

Diana smiled. "If they are able to find their way through that part of my defenses in less than a year or two I shall be astonished," she said. "And as for Darr, you're continually getting parcels of queer stuff from all over the world."

"But not a great deal of it is lichens, unfortunately," Francis told her. "Naturally, I was careful and took precautions against accidents, but an intensive investigation is rather a different matter...." He shrugged uncertainly.

"Even so," Diana said, "who's going to identify the particular species of lichen? We gave it a nice long name, but the only people who can say which plant the name belongs to is us—you and I."

"If they find the collectors, they are not going to have much trouble in discovering which lichen they've been collecting," Francis pointed out.

They sat in thoughtful silence while the waiter fussed, and refilled their glasses. Francis broke it to say, philosophically:

"It had to come, Diana. One's always known it must, sooner or later."

"I'd rather have had longer," Diana said, frowning, "but I suppose I'd feel like that whenever it came. Just that damned Wilberry woman and her allergy . . . It can't be a common allergy, either, or I should have met it before. Still, it can't be helped now." She was silent again for a moment. Then she went on:

"We've kept saying 'they.' Have we any idea who 'they' may be?"

Francis shrugged.

"No telling. No reputable firm would touch it in the circumstances. But the Saxover name would get her a hearing anywhere else in the trade."

"Yes. I suppose it would be in the trade?"

"I should say so. It would be unlike Jane to pay unnecessary commission to an intermediary."

Diana frowned. She told him:

"I'm growing to like this still less, Francis. There could be ways of handling it that would be fantastically profitable . . . while they lasted." She gave a rueful smile. "After all, I haven't done so badly myself—but if one had had no scruples . . . !" She let that drop, and continued: "A plain leak was one thing, but this is different, I mean, if *they* have no scruples about how they get hold of it, they're not going to have many when they're sure there's a chance of making billions out of it."

Francis shook his head.

"They won't be able to hold it—whoever 'they' are," he said. "Look at what's happened just because I told my own son and daughter."

"Possibly," she agreed. "But what I meant is that it might be as well to spike them now, by publishing. Once they're convinced that it is the real thing, their quickest way to get more is to steal it, and the process, too, if they can—or, better still, to kidnap one, or both, of us."

"That's something I did think of," Francis told her. "There's nothing to be found at Darr now, and, if I should disappear, publication will follow automatically. I imagine you will have taken similar precautions?"

Diana nodded.

They regarded one another, across the coffee cups.

"Oh, Francis," she said. "This is so damned silly, and petty. All we want to do is to *give* people something. To make an old, old dream come true. We can offer them life, with time to live it; instead of a quick scrabble for existence, and finish. Time to grow wise enough to build a new world. Time to become full men and women instead of overgrown children. And look at us—you hamstrung by the prospect of chaos; me, sure they will try to counter that prospect by suppression. Both of us still on the same old stands."

She poured herself another cup of coffee. For nearly a minute she sat peering into it as if it were a dark crystal. Then she looked up.

"It has gone too far, Francis. We can't hold it any longer. Will you publish?"

"Not yet," Francis told her.

"I warn you, I shall begin to prepare my ladies."

"You might as well," he agreed. "That is different from making a scientific announcement that one knows cannot be implemented."

"It will be implemented if they demand it loudly enough." She paused. "No, you're right, Francis, it will be more effective if you come in later—but I have offered."

"I won't forget, Diana."

"In a little while I'll brief my nine hundred and eighty ladies more thoroughly, and turn them loose to fight. I don't see them taking the threat of suppression quietly." She paused again, and then laughed. "What a pity my militant Great-Aunt Anne can't be here. She'd be in her element. Hammer for the shop-windows, petrol for the letter-boxes, scenes in the House! She'd enjoy that."

"You're looking forward to it," Francis told her, disapprovingly.

"Of course I am," said Diana. "Strategically, I could still do with more time, but personally—well, if you'd spent twelve years working for it, embroiled in a pink-shaded, flower-scented, soft-carpeted, silk-bowed, Cellophane-protected dreamland populated by purring, scheming, hard-eyed, grasping, cynical, retractible-clawed bitches who support themselves by assisting other women to employ their secondary sexual characteristics to the best advantage, you'd welcome pretty nearly any kind of change, too."

Francis laughed.

"But I'm told you're no mean businesswoman," he said.

"That side of it can be tolerably amusing for a time," Diana admitted, "and profitable, too. But as I do provide something that my rivals only purport to provide, I could scarcely go wrong, could I?"

"And the future?—After all, you'll have quite a lot of future."

Diana said, lightly:

"I have my plans—Plan A, Plan B, Plan C. Now that's enough about me. I want to know what's been happening to you, and to Darr, all this long time. . . ."

Part THREE

9

Diana paused as she passed through the outer office, on her way to her own.

"Good morning, Sarah. Is there anything special today?"

"Not in the mail, Miss Brackley," Miss Tallwyn told her. "But there's this. I don't suppose you'll have seen it yet." She held open a copy of *The Reflector*. As usual, it looked more like a printer's pie than a layout. Heavy crossheads dominated a jumble of boxes and fancy rules littered with a dozen different faces and sizes of type. In contrast, the quarter-page advertisement indicated by Miss Tallwyn's thumb attained distinction.

"BEAUTY!" it announced. "Beauty that lasts! Beauty that is *more* than skin-deep! From the sea, the great mother of all living things, we bring you new, deeper beauty—beauty with GLAMARE! GLAMARE is glamour fetched from the sea to your own dressing-table. You'll find the true, tangy, exciting astringency of the sea-wind in GLAMARE!

"Out of all the substances held in solution in the sea, just *one* particular sea-plant selects, absorbs, and concentrates those which hold the secret of lasting, deep-reaching beauty. Thanks to the work of skilled chemists and eminent beauticians the miracle essence of this plant, hitherto the costly prerogative of a world-famed luxury beauty salon, is now available to YOU ...

"GLAMARE is not superficial. A sense of *inner* beauty will ..."

"Ah, well," said Diana. "Just about a month from the starting pistol. Not at all bad going."

"According to *my* information all Galway seaweed is still tied up while the Irish government tries to find out which is the important kind of weed, and to decide how much export duty to levy on it," said Miss Tallwyn.

"Sarah, dear, how long have you been in this enterprising trade?" Diana inquired.

"I am not in it," said Miss Tallwyn. "I am your secretary."

"You'd not be interested in a bet that two days after the ban is lifted there'll be another lot along claiming to use only genuine original Galway weed?"

"I never gamble," said Miss Tallwyn.

"Lots of people think they don't," Diana told her. "Well, now, anything else?"

"Miss Brendon would like to see you."

Diana nodded.

"Tell her to come up as soon as she's free."

"And Lady Tewley wishes to make an appointment."

"But—oh, with me personally, you mean. Why?"

"She said it was a personal matter. She was very insistent. I arranged provisionally for three o'clock. I can cancel if you like."

Diana shook her head.

"No. Confirm it, Sarah. Lady Tewley wouldn't insist without good cause."

Diana went on into her own office. She busied herself there with several letters Miss Tallwyn had left ready. After a quarter of an hour or so Miss Brendon was shown in.

"Good morning, Lucy. Sit down. How is the Brendon Secret Service going?"

"Well, Miss Brackley, one of its interesting discoveries is that it isn't the only secret service you operate here. I think you might have told me about that—or them about me. It's been awkward, once or twice."

"Oh, you've run across Tania's network, have you? Don't worry, my dear. Their function is different; more of a C.I.D. nature. But I'll have a word with Tania. We don't want you wasting your time investigating one another. But what else?"

Miss Brendon frowned a little.

"It's not easy to sort it out," she said, "so many people seem to be interested. There's the man Marlin from the *Prole*. He cropped up again and has offered me fifty pounds if I can get him a specimen of the actual seaweed we use. . . ."

"He's getting rash," Diana put in. "How would he be knowing it wasn't any old kind of weed?"

"Well, in his place, I'd get to know just what kinds are found in Galway Bay, and what kinds are common elsewhere. That should narrow it down to just a few possible kinds, anyway. And if I were to give him any other he'd know right off it was an attempted bluff."

"Yes, I'll think about that. Go on," Diana told her.

"Then, from him, I learned that the police are interested. There's been an inspector asking him questions about us, and making inquiries from that allergy woman, Mrs. Wilberry, too. His name is Averhouse, and according to the *Prole*'s crime reporter he's usually to be found on narcotics cases. Also, he was accompanied by a Sergeant Moyne—and it happens that Averil Todd who works on the ground floor has been taken up by a young man called Moyne, who *says* he's in the Civil Service."

"The *Prole*, and the police. Who else?" Diana asked.

"The man from the *Radar*, Freddy Rammer, is still working on Bessie Holt, who can't tell him anything, but is still hopefully stringing him along, and getting free dinners out of it. Several other girls have acquired new boy-friends, some of whom are definitely connected with cosmetics firms, others may be, but no details yet."

"What a hive of curiosity we are," said Diana. "All of them out to identify the particular seaweed?"

"Most," agreed Miss Brendon. "But I don't quite see why the police should bother about that. And, by the way, a day or two after Inspector Averhouse called on her, Mrs. Wilberry went to a man in Harley Street, apparently for a check-up."

"The dear police, so conventional. However, I don't think we need to worry about peddling. We put the fear of God into the girls over that kind of thing, as you know, and Tania's lot watch for any sign of it like hawks—and not only among the staff." She paused. "On the other hand, there is just a chance, I suppose, that they're imagining something else than dope this time. If you can find out what they're after, and it isn't dope, I'll be glad to know."

"I'll do my best, Miss Brackley," said Miss Brendon, preparing to get up.

Diana checked her with a gesture. She looked at her long and thoughtfully until Miss Brendon went a little pink.

"If there's nothing more—" she began.

Diana cut her short.

"There is, Lucy. Something important. The time is coming when I shall need someone close to me whom I can trust. I'm going to make you an offer. I know quite a lot about you, more, probably, than you imagine. You told me why you came here; and I have, I fancy, a pretty good idea what you think of this place. Now, I want to tell you some things that no one here knows about, no one but me, and then make you a proposition."

Diana got up and slid across a small bolt on each of the doors. She went back to her desk, and picked up the telephone.

"No calls until I tell you, please, Sarah," she said, and put the receiver back.

"Now ..." she began....

—

Promptly at three o'clock Miss Tallwyn opened the door to announce: "Lady Tewley, Miss Brackley."

Lady Tewley entered. She was tall, slim, and elegant in a soft leather suit of a delicate gray. Everything from the points of her shoes to the crown of her small hat was carefully considered in each particular, other than cost, and she did credit to all her producers, including Nefertiti Ltd.

Diana waited until the door closed. She said:

"Janet, my dear, you disturb me. I have only to see you, and I begin to wonder whether I don't make some slight contribution to an art-form after all."

Lady Tewley wrinkled her nose at her.

"Coming from you, Diana, that's close to fishing. But it really is rather nice, isn't it?" She looked down at herself with approval. "And, after all, the unemployed must occupy themselves somehow."

She sat down gracefully. Diana offered her the cigarette box, and flicked the table-lighter. Janet Tewley blew out a plume of smoke, and leaned back a little. They looked at one another. Janet Tewley chuckled.

"I know what you're thinking, Diana, and it's very flattering of you to look so smug about it."

Diana smiled. She had indeed been thinking of their first meeting, ten years ago. The Lady Tewley who had looked at her across this same desk then had been very different. A tall nervous girl of twenty-two, with good looks, a lovely figure and limbs, no idea of dress, a sketch of a make-up, an utterly unsuitable hair style, and a disposition to gangle like a sixteen year old. She had looked at Diana solemnly and carefully, and ended by saying: "Oh, good," apparently to herself, and with a slightly surprised air. Diana's mouth had twitched a little at the corners as she raised her eyebrows.

The girl looked somewhat confused.

"I'm sorry," she said, "I didn't mean to be rude. But I've never been in a place like this before," she added ingenuously. "I had an idea it would be run by someone about sixty with tinted hair, an enameled face, tight corsets, like a sort of toughened-up Queen Victoria."

"But in spite of that, you came here," said Diana. "I'm glad to be a weight off your mind. Now, what do you want me to do?"

The girl hesitated briefly. Then she said:

"A sort of Pygmalion thing." Confidingly she went on:

"You see, I've—I've taken on the job of being Lady Tewley, and it's only fair that I should try to do it properly. It isn't the kind of thing I ever expected, so I need help. I—" she hesitated again, "I don't much care for the kind of help I've been offered. So I thought I could get it from someone who is professional, disinterested—" She let the sentence hang, unfinished.

Diana had a brief vision of sisters-in-law, and aunts-in-law applying themselves to the work with little tact. The girl added: "I can learn, and I think I could look right, but I haven't had the right kind of apprenticeship. It isn't a thing I ever had time to bother about much."

Diana told her frankly:

"You could certainly look right. I can see to it that you do. I can recommend you good guides and tutors, too. How much you learn from them will be your own affair."

"I can learn," the girl repeated. "What I need now is a good grounding in the grammar of it. And if I can't soon beat some of these nitwits at their own game, then I'll deserve what I get."

Diana nodded slowly.

"I understand you," she said. "But you mustn't underestimate them. They're on their home territory, and they are pretty single-minded about their social lives—after all, they're all they've got.

It's one thing to do your job, but you're not doing it well if you break your heart."

"I shan't break my heart. I've no ambition to climb. If I had, I'd use it on something worth climbing," the girl assured her. "But I took this on, and it's up to me to be an asset, not a liability, that's all."

She spoke with a touch of bitterness. Diana noticed that her eyes had become a little shinier than before. She asked, curiously:

"What were you doing before?"

"Six months ago I was a fourth-year medical, living in a bedsitter in Bloomsbury," Lady Tewley told her. "I knew the requirements there. I didn't know these would turn out to be quite so different."

Diana had speculated for a moment on the circumstances which lay behind the girl's thorough change of milieu. She said forthrightly:

"I see no reason why you should not make a success of it. In fact, I am sure you can if you set your mind to it. But you will find that it isn't cheap."

"I didn't suppose so," Lady Tewley replied. "That's one of my early lessons—you owe it to your self-respect to spend a lot of money on yourself, not to do that is bourgeois."

"Very well, then," Diana agreed. And they had gone ahead.

Seeing the impeccably dressed, carefully mannered, and assured Lady Tewley before her now, she smiled a little at the recollection of the girl who had come asking her help.

"Smug is the wrong word," she said. "Pleasurable satisfaction—and admiration—would be nearer."

"I take them in," conceded Janet Tewley, modestly. "Though I say it myself, I can give a pretty good imitation when required."

"But it remains an imitation? No mutation?"

"My dear Diana, you, of all people, ought to be aware of an imitation when you see one. That's what used to puzzle me so much about you. I do my imitation because I married into circumstances which require it. But why, I used to ask myself, does Diana do hers? And I couldn't find an answer."

"Used to?" Diana repeated. "Don't you now?"

"Well, a continuously unanswered question can grow tedious, can't it?" Janet Tewley said evasively. "However, you'll want to know what I came about."

Diana nodded.

"I'm afraid it isn't very pleasant," Janet went on. "Our rather chic and expensive set is about as full of monotonously dirty washing as a laundry on Mondays, as you can scarcely fail to know."

"In a general way, yes," Diana admitted.

"That's what I admire about you, Diana. I imagine that practically every member of your staff knows every sordid detail, and you just don't bother with them."

"Should I?"

"Well, considering that you preside over this gossip-exchange . . . Anyway, I take it you won't have heard about my affair with a Mr. Smelton yet?"

Diana shook her head.

Janet rummaged in the bag that exactly matched her suit. Presently she produced a flexible gold bracelet set with diamonds, and placed it on Diana's desk, where it twinkled lustrously.

"Nice, isn't it—Horace Smelton gave it to me for my birthday. It's what fishermen call a spinner, I think—or do I mean a spoon? Anyway, one of those things one is supposed to gobble up . . ." She regarded it reflectively. "The funny thing is," she went on, "that although it was Horace who gave it to me, it was my husband who bought it. I just happened to find that out. And it was my husband who introduced Horace to me about a couple of months ago ...

"I don't want to make a long saga of this, but your staff probably know, if you don't, that my husband and I have been on, well, just formal terms for nearly three years now. We put up a show in public, but that's about all. So what, I wondered, was going on?

"At first glance one might think he wanted to land me in a mess for purposes of divorce. He isn't a very nice man, you know. But when I thought it over, there were several reasons why that wouldn't do. So I decided to try to discover the real reason. It seemed to me that there must be something he wanted to find out, but since we are practically not on speaking terms in private, it wasn't much good his asking me anything directly. Well, Horace is quite an attractive man, even if he is a snake in the grass, so I played along—not too much encouragement, but no definite repulse."

Janet Tewley dropped the end of her cigarette into the ashtray, and lit another.

"To cut it short," she resumed, "I noticed that Nefertiti seemed to be cropping up in our conversations now and then. Oh, Horace is quite subtle, but I was watching for any recurring theme, so I tried a ploy or two, and praised the results of your seaweed discovery. He played it gently. He didn't immediately say that the stuff about seaweed was sheer eyewash; he just let that come out later. In due course, we got around to a proposition. If we could get hold of specimens of all the various things you use in Nefertiti, particularly anything that is injected, he knew of people who would be willing to give a good price for them. If I could induce one of your girls to tell me anything about your raw materials, that would be valuable, too. If she could get me a little, even a small fragment, of a particular raw material, one that would very likely look like a bit of lichen, they would pay a very good price indeed.

"When I thought that over, I remembered that Alec, my husband, has a very old friend who is a director of Sandworth Chemical Products, Limited."

Janet paused again, and shook her head gently.

"In fact, Diana, I have an impression that the jig is very nearly up."

Diana looked at her steadily.

"The jig?" she inquired.

"My dear," said Janet. "I have known you now for ten years. In all that time both of us have changed quite remarkably little, don't you think? Besides, I did do four years of medicine, you remember. I'm possibly the only client of yours who has. Interesting. In fact, I rather think that if what I am thinking is right, I might take it up again. It's nice to have nice clothes and so on, but the cost of this kind of life is rather higher than I care for. Besides, it would be so boring for any length of time, don't you think?"

Diana kept her gaze level and steady.

"How long have you been thinking what you think, Janet?"

Lady Tewley shrugged.

"It is difficult to say, my dear, partly because it is so difficult to accept. The best I can tell you is that my suspicions solidified into a conviction about three years ago."

"But you didn't tell anyone?"

"No. I was fascinated. I wanted to see what would happen. After all, if I was right, I had plenty of time to wait; if I was wrong, it didn't matter, anyway. I know you, Diana. I trust you. There was no real reason for me to interfere—until now. Now that I have, I'm bursting with questions, of course."

Diana looked at her. Janet Tewley had accommodated her

manner to her environment too successfully to display anything but a graceful lassitude. Diana smiled, and glanced at her clock.

"Very well," she agreed, "but only half an hour, now."

"A cardinal one first, then," said Janet. "Is the retarding action followed by a corresponding acceleration of deterioration if the treatment is discontinued?"

"No," Diana told her. "Metabolism merely returns to normal."

"That's a relief. I've been a bit haunted by the idea that one day I might have to go from middle-age to senility in about five minutes. Now, about secondary effects, and response to stimuli. I've wondered whether I haven't detected . . . ?"

The questions continued for more than half an hour until they were interrupted by a ringing of the telephone. Diana picked it up. Miss Tallwyn's voice said:

"I'm sorry, Miss Brackley. I know you didn't want to be disturbed, but Miss Saxover is on the line, for the third time. She says it is very urgent and important."

"Very well, Sarah. Put her through."

Diana waved down Lady Tewley, who was preparing to leave.

"Hullo, Zephanie. What is it?"

"It's about Darr, Diana," Zephanie's voice told her. "Daddy thought it wiser not to ring you himself."

"What's happened?"

"There's been a fire. The living wing is practically burnt out. Daddy had a narrow escape."

"But he's all right?" Diana asked, anxiously.

"Oh yes. He was able to get up on the roof of the wing, and across to the main building. They managed to confine the fire to the wing, but what he's anxious for you to know is that the police are quite sure the fire was started deliberately."

"But who would want to do that? There'd be no object—"

"He says the police think it was very likely that there was an attempt at burglary first, and the fire was started afterward to cover up. They say they've found traces of that. It's impossible, of course, to know what they may have taken. But I'm to tell you not to worry about you-know-what. There was nothing there that had anything to do with that."

"I see, Zephanie, that's good. But your father. You are perfectly sure he's not hurt?"

"No, really, Diana. He says all that happened to him was that he grazed one knee, and ruined his pajamas."

"Thank goodness for that," Diana said.

After a few more sentences she put back the receiver with a hand that shook slightly. For nearly half a minute she stared blankly at the opposite wall until a movement by Janet Tewley recalled her.

"There are too many of them getting too close," she said, half to herself. "It's time to move— No, don't go, Janet. I'll have a job for you. Just a minute . . ."

She picked up the telephone again.

"Sarah. You know that parcel in the corner of the big safe?— yes, that's it. You'll find it's full of letters. They're already addressed and stamped. Please see that they are put in the post straight away. They must go off tonight."

She turned back to Janet Tewley.

"This," she said, "is where we take the lid off. Those letters are invitations to all my clients, and to some of the Press, to attend a meeting next Wednesday afternoon—more than a thousand altogether. I've tried to make them seem important and urgent, but unfortunately they have to be a circular letter—which means that some people will disregard them, and others will think them some kind of publicity stuff. Now, you know quite a lot of the clients socially. What I'd like you to do is start a rumor going that will back up the letter, and fetch them here. I shall get the girls down below to help, too. But if you'll spread it from outside it will carry more weight."

"Very well," Janet agreed. "But what's the rumor? You won't want the real thing out before the meeting, will you?"

"Oh, certainly not. No, we'd better keep to the seaweed for the moment. What about all our work here being threatened, our clients in danger of being deprived of our services, because the Irish are fixing the duty on our essential kind of seaweed so high that the Board of Trade refuses to sanction payments at these extortionate rates? This will be a protest meeting against a discriminatory ruling which is backed by rival concerns, and aimed at depriving Nefertiti clients of their special benefits. Do you think something along those lines?"

Janet nodded. "I think so. There's room for embroidery. Suggestions that the Board of Trade, or the Bank of England, or something, has been got at by rival interests. It's all part of a dark takeover plot by people who don't give a damn what happens to your clients as long as they gain control of Nefertiti Ltd, and your trade secrets. Yes, I think it ought to stir up quite a sense of injustice."

"All right then, Janet. You set that going. I'll arrange a leak to the staff here—it's much more effective than telling them anything directly—and we'll hope for a good full hall on Wednesday."

10

A black saloon car tore past them, and cut in ahead. A panel bearing the word "Police" flashed on. An arm protruding from the driver's window waved them down.

"What the devil—?" said Richard, as he slowed.

"But we weren't *doing* anything, were we?" Zephanie asked, in bewilderment.

A moment after they had stopped another vehicle drew up alongside, a small van with no lettering on it. The nearside door of the van opened, and a man got out. He looked to the rear.

"Right, Charlie?" he called.

"Okay," said a voice.

The man put his hand in his pocket. At the same time he jerked open the door beside Richard, and held up a pistol.

"Out!" he said.

The door on the other side opened just as suddenly. Another man said "Out!" to Zephanie.

"Into the van," he added, thrusting forward his pistol.

Zephanie opened her mouth to speak.

"Shut up. Get in," he told her.

There was a sharp crack from a pistol on Richard's side of the car.

"See? It works. Come on now," said the first man.

Richard and Zephanie, each with a pistol pressing their backs, were shepherded to the rear, and into the van. The two men climbed in after them and shut the door. It was all over inside half a minute.

———

The room was large. The furniture was old-fashioned, comfortable, but shabby. The man who sat behind the leather-topped desk had turned the lamp so that it shone in Zephanie's eyes, and left his own face a pale blur in the shadow. She stood a little to his right, with one of the men from the van close behind her. Richard stood a little to the left, his hands bound behind him, a piece of plaster across his mouth, and the other man watchfully beside him.

"There is no malice in this, Miss Saxover," said the man behind the desk. "I simply want some information from you, and I intend to get it. It will be much pleasanter for everybody if you answer my questions truthfully straight off." He paused, the half-seen splodge of pale face still turned toward her. "Now," he went on, "your father has made a very remarkable discovery. I am sure you know what I mean."

"My father has made a lot of important discoveries," Zephanie said.

The man's left hand tapped the desk. . . . The man standing beside Richard clenched his fist, and made a short powerful jab at Richard's stomach. Richard gave a muffled gasp, and folded forward.

"Let's not waste time," said the man at the desk. "You tell me which discovery I mean."

Zephanie looked round helplessly. She made to move, but two hands from behind grasped her upper arms firmly. She kicked back with her heel. The man promptly stamped agonizing on her other foot. Before she could recover he had pulled off both her shoes, and thrown them away.

The man at the desk tapped his left hand again. A fist thudded against Richard's head.

"We have no wish to harm you if it can be helped, Miss Saxover," said the man at the desk, "but we don't much mind how far we have to go with your friend here. However, if you don't much mind that either, it will be very unpleasant for him, and we shall have to proceed to direct methods with you, yourself. And if you are obstinate we shall have to persuade your father to tell us. Do you think that if he were to receive that ring of yours—with your finger still inside it, of course—he would be willing to cooperate?" He paused again. "Now, Miss Saxover, you were about to tell me which discovery I mean."

Zephanie set her teeth, and shook her head. There was another thud on her right, and a groan. She trembled. Another thud.

"Oh, God! Oh, stop it!" she cried.

"It's in your hands," said the man at the desk.

"You mean—living longer. . . ." she said, wretchedly.

"That's better," he told her. "And the drug used is an extract of . . . what? Please don't say seaweed. You'll only hurt your friend."

Zephanie hesitated wretchedly. She saw the fingers of his left hand rise to tap.

"Lichen. It's lichen," she told him.

"Quite right, Miss Saxover. You do know the answers, you see. Now, this particular lichen, what is it called?"

"I can't tell you," she said. "No, no, don't hit him. I *can't* tell you. It hasn't got a proper name. It isn't classified."

The man at the desk considered, and decided to accept that.

"What does it look like? Describe it."

"I can't," she told him. "I've never seen it." She shuddered at the sound of another blow. "Oh, don't—don't. I *can't* tell you. Oh, stop him. You must believe me. I don't know!"

The man held up his left hand. The thuds stopped, and there was only the sound of groans from Richard, and of his half-strangled breathing. Zephanie dared not look at him. She faced the desk with tears running down her cheeks. The man behind it opened a drawer, and took out a card. It had specimens of a dozen or more kinds of lichen glued to it.

"Which of these classes does it most closely resemble?" he asked.

Zephanie shook her head helplessly.

"I don't know. I tell you, I've never seen it. I *can't* tell. Oh, Richard. Oh, God! Stop it, stop it! He said it was an *imperfectus*. That's all I can tell you."

"There are hundreds of lichens *imperfecti*."

"I know. But that's all I can tell you. I swear it is."

"Very well, we'll leave that for the moment, and turn to another question. I'd like you, bearing in mind that you don't quite know how much I know and the unpleasant consequences that lies will bring to your friend here, I'd like you to tell me where your father gets the lichen from . . . ?"

—

"No, she's all right—physically. They didn't harm her," Francis's voice said. "But, of course, she's badly shocked and distressed."

"Poor Zephanie, I should think so," Diana said into the telephone. "How's the young man—Richard?"

"Pretty badly knocked about, I'm afraid. Zephanie says when she came round they were lying on the grass verge beside the car which was still where they'd stopped. It was just getting light and poor Richard looked a frightful mess. A farmhand came along, and they got him into the car between them, and she took him to hospital. They said there that it looked worse than it was. He's lost a few teeth, but there's no serious injury, as far as they could tell without an X-ray. So she came on here to Darr by herself. The chief trouble is that she's in such a state about it. But what could she do? She didn't know when they were trapping her into a lie, and when they genuinely didn't know the answer. And each time she lied he suffered. I've no doubt they'd have beaten her up, too, if she'd held out."

"Poor child. How much did she tell them?" Diana asked.

"Pretty much everything she knew, I think—except that your side of it was never raised at all."

"But they know where we get it now?"

"Yes. I'm afraid they do."

"Oh, dear. That's my fault. I should never have told her. I hope it doesn't start serious trouble. Still, it can't be helped. Do try to reassure her as much as you can. I suppose you've no idea who this lot could be?"

"No way of telling," Francis said.

"They can scarcely be your daughter-in-law's friends, could they? My name would be almost bound to have cropped up if they were. It could be anybody. There seem to be half-a-dozen on the scent now, not counting the newspapers and the police. I'm telling the clients and the Press at the meeting on Wednesday, you know. It doesn't look as if it would hold up more than a few days, anyway."

There was silence at the other end of the telephone.

"You're still there?" Diana asked.

"Yes," said Francis's voice.

"Look Francis, I don't want to hog this. You know that. We *both* worked it out. Won't you let me tell them so?"

"I still think it's better not—not at first. . . ."

"But—"

"My dear, it's now a matter of tactics. What you are doing is, frankly, starting a sensation on a popular level. It is going to be regarded by responsible people as an advertisement for your firm, a publicity stunt."

"Possibly, just at first—but not for long."

"I still think I'd be of more value among the reserves."

Diana was silent for a moment.

"Very well, Francis. But I wish—oh, well."

"Diana, do be careful—of yourself, I mean. A lot of people are going to get very worked up about this."

"Don't worry about me, Francis. I know what I'm doing."

"I'm not at all sure that you do, my dear."

"Francis, this is what I've been working for. The idea of an antigerone must be put over. They must *demand* it . . ."

"Very well. It's too late to stop now. But I repeat, please do be careful, Diana. . . ."

11

On Thursday morning Diana tackled a stack of newspapers with the avidity of a rising star after a first night. As she continued to work through them, however, her eagerness wilted.

The Times had nothing—well, you'd scarcely expect quick-off-the-mark stuff from old sobersides. Nothing in the *Guardian* either. Nor in the *Telegraph*—which was a bit queer; hang it, there had been quite a good showing of titles at the meeting. A small paragraph on the woman's page of the *News Chronicle* mentioned that a famous Mayfair beauty-specialist had announced a new treatment, claiming unusual efficacy in the preservation of youthful beauty. The *Mail* said:

> If the example of a famous west-end beauty house, which has announced its new treatment with all the éclat of a dress-designer showing his season's collection, is going to be widely followed, I can foresee a time when we shall be treated to parades of the coming fashions in autumn and spring faces by our leading beauticians.

The *Express* remarked:

> Modesty was never a noticeable characteristic of the beauty business, and it was certainly not there to check the claims made by a well-known expert yesterday when she addressed an audience of Mayfair's feminine élite. It is not to be denied

that much that can be done, and is done, for the female face and figure makes the world a brighter place, but exaggerated promises can only result in a wave of disappointment which will break over the head of the maker.

A paragraph in the *Mirror* under the heading: AFTER SEA-WEED? commented:

Those of our readers who have been disappointed by the miraculous powers attributed to, but not so far shown by, seaweed need not give up hope. Yesterday came another red-hot tip (from the same high-toned beauty stable) for irresistible glamour. The successes claimed for the new treatment are even more impressive—it isn't seaweed any longer; in fact, it is not clear what it is, but it will cost you two or three hundred pounds to back it and see what happens.

The *Herald* showed concern along similar lines:

A TEENAGER AT FORTY?

Women who have the luck to be married to a good expense-account will be rejoicing today. From perfumed Mayfair comes the good news that the doors of eternal youth will be opened to them at the cost of a mere three or four hundred pounds a year. No doubt with the present distribution of wealth in this country the capitalists who have launched this enterprise will rejoice, too. Many will feel that there are ways in which eight pounds a week could bring more benefit to the community than this, but as long as the present Tory government....

And the *Sketch*:

You're only young once, they say. But, according to an expert in the glamour business, that's out of date. The modern miss can be young twice, or three times—if she likes. All she has to do is to call in the help of science—and pay a thumping fee, of course. For our part, we have an idea the same offer was being made before science was even thought of; and probably on the same terms.

"Very disappointing," said Miss Tallwyn, with sympathy. "If only you had been able to give it some news-value," she added.

Diana stared at her.

"Good heavens, Sarah! What *do* you mean? It's the greatest news since—since Adam!"

Miss Tallwyn shook her head again.

"News, and news-value, aren't the same thing," she said. "They've decided it's a publicity stunt, I'm afraid. And there's nothing that terrifies the British Press more than the risk of giving a free advertisement."

"They've just wilfully pretended not to understand it. The clients understood it all right, most of them. And, God knows, I made it plain enough," Diana protested.

"You've lived with it a long time, you're used to it. They aren't. As for the clients—well, a lot of them must have been wondering a bit already, you know, one way and another—they were ready for an explanation, wanting it, in fact. But the journalists! Well, put yourself in their place, Miss Brackley. They're sent off to cover what appears to be a business-sponsored keep-your-beauty lecture good for a paragraph or two on the woman's page. I won't say that you didn't probably set a few of them thinking a bit, and you may have prepared the ground, too. But how do you imagine they're going to get what you really told them past a hard-boiled editor? I know. I had some of it at one time. What you need now is something sensational—"

"For goodness' sake, Sarah. If what I told them isn't—"

"Sensational, in the newspaper sense, I mean. A good fast jab at the superficial emotions. What you gave us was just a sinker-in; a lot of implications that take time to register."

Diana said, a little more hopefully:

"Perhaps it was naïve to expect an immediate explosion. But there are the Sundays to come yet. They'll have had more time to realize it—and it could be very much their kind of thing, couldn't it? I don't much mind *how* they handle it, as long as they don't ignore it. And then, of course, there are the women's weeklies, and the monthlies. . . . Some of them are *bound* to make a thing of it, surely. . . ."

But as things turned out Diana did not have to wait for either the Sundays or the weeklies, for it was on the afternoon of that same Thursday, just after the Stock Exchange had closed, that The Threadneedle and Western Assurance Company declared a moratorium on the payment of annuities and guaranteed incomes, until further notice. They described the step as "a purely temporary measure undertaken with regret pending legal opinion upon the obligations of the Company in cases where means have been employed to extend the normal expectation of life."

In the opinion of many, particularly that of stockholders in the T. & W.A.C., and certain other insurance companies, temporary or not, it was a damnfool measure to take. "Why," muttered indignant voices, "why did the half-wits on the board have to shoot their mouths off in public? Even if there's anything in it, it couldn't have cost them much to keep quiet about it until they *had taken* counsel's opinion, the silly bees."

On Friday, Threadneedle and Western opened five shillings down. A rumor raced round the market that a certain Q.C. had been heard to state in the National Liberal Club the previous evening that as it was already an important part of a doctor's function to extend lives threatened with extinction, and one that was practiced daily, he entirely failed to see that any question should arise. Neither God, nor the Law, was aware of an obligation to justify an actuary's figures for him. And while the term "his natural life" might raise some speculation regarding the nature of "unnatural life," life continued, for the reasonable man, to mean that life had not been terminated by death.

Insurance stocks drifted lower.

Arguments as to whether there was anything at all in this "extension of life business" washed back and forth, uncertainly. A feeling that the whole thing had been grossly exaggerated began to spread.

Insurance stocks steadied.

Three minor companies followed the example of Threadneedle and Western, and announced moratoria. So perhaps there was more in it than one had thought.

Insurance stocks started down again.

About two o'clock in the afternoon a Late Night Final edition of an evening paper arrived. On the City page it recorded:

Yesterday's announcement of a temporary moratorium on certain payments by Threadneedle and Western led to unsettled conditions on the London Stock Exchange today. Insurances opened torpid and glissaded slowly lower. Later a slight revigoration set in and they sobered with dominant issues a few shillings slimmer. Fidelity, however, was not nourished, and, later, prices once more verged into a slow sink.

The unusual step taken by Threadneedle and Western is attributed to an announcement made last Wednesday by Miss Diana Brackley, who controls the well-known West-end beauty salons of Nefertiti Ltd, in which she claimed that definite progress had been achieved in slowing the natural rate of organic deterioration, which would lead to a perceptible rise in the present figures for the expectation of life.

The fact that this claim has evidently received more serious attention in actuarial circles than would seem likely to be given to an announcement emanating from such a source is probably attributable to the fact that Miss Brackley is a scientist, holding high honours in biochemistry from Cambridge University, who spent several years in advanced biochemical research work before turning her talents to the development of her notably successful business in a field where competition is notoriously strong and custom proverbially fickle....

One young man, frowning slightly, pointed the paragraph out to his colleague.

"In other words she's probably got something. 'Perceptible rise in the expectation' doesn't tell us much, but it seems to have been enough to put the wind up Threadneedle, and the others. I reckon we might sell those General Eventualities before the going gets rough."

It was not an isolated decision.

The going got rough.

—

The Times restricted its comments to the financial page, and the effects on insurance stocks. Without specifying the cause, it reproved those who had allowed their judgment to be stampeded by unsubstantial rumors, and had thereby encouraged panicky reactions in what was normally one of the most stable sections of the market.

The *Financial Times* was more factual, but also cautious. It, too, deplored the effect of a possibly irresponsible announcement, but it also drew attention to the noticeable rise in chemicals, particularly United Commonwealth Chemicals' ordinaries, which had set in at approximately the same time that insurances began their second decline. The *Express,* the *Mail,* the *News Chronicle* all made references to Miss Brackley's claims, but preserved a careful vagueness on details—there was, for instance, no suggested figure of the life-increase; just an indefinite proposition that people might be able to live a little longer—and in each case it was given a not-too-committal position of only semi-validity, on the woman's page.

The *Mirror,* however, had pulled off something better. It had discovered that Mrs. Joseph Macmartin (or Mrs. Margaret Macmartin, as it more chummily preferred to call her), the wife of the Chairman of the board of Threadneedle and Western Assurance, was a Nefertiti client of eight years' standing. It printed its own photograph of Mrs. Macmartin alongside one alleged to have been taken ten years ago. The lack of difference was impressive. She was quoted as saying: "I do not have a moment's doubt of the sincerity of Miss Brackley's claims. Nor am I alone in this. Hundreds of women whose lives have been revolutionized by her discovery are just as grateful to her as I am." Even so, there was again a disinclination to particularize on details of the claims.

The *Telegraph* had interviewed Lady Tewley who appeared to have said, no doubt among other things, "Nature is unfair to women. We flower with tragic brevity. Hitherto, science which has transformed the world has neglected us, but now comes Miss Brackley like a messenger from Olympus, offering us what every woman desires—a long summer of full bloom. It seems likely that this will lead to a fall in the present rate of divorce."

Diana started Saturday by granting requests for interviews. Mounting pressure, however, caused her to abandon her piecemeal approach, and arrange a full-scale Press conference. It was a gathering which started with a high content of cynicism, flippancy, and a peppering of ribaldry. She grew a little short with it, and broke off her introduction to say:

"Look here, *I* didn't promote this meeting. It was *you* who were anxious to meet me. I'm not trying to sell you anything. I don't give a damn whether you believe what I say, or not. It doesn't make any difference to the facts. If you like to go away and cleverly take the mickey out of it, you can—though it will be your faces that get red, not mine. But, for the present, let's get on with it. You ask the questions: I'll give you some of the answers."

Nobody convinces a gathering of the Press one hundred percent, and success is further weakened when one refuses to answer several crucial questions. Nevertheless, when the representatives dispersed several of them were looking more subdued and thoughtful than they had when they arrived.

It was difficult to tell which of Sunday's papers had rejected it, and which had considered it unworthy of disturbing their planned layouts. Some gave it a guarded mention but neither the *Prole* nor the *Radar* had doubts of its readability; in their later editions they changed the make-up, and went to town on it. DOES A WOMAN *WANT* TO LIVE 200 YEARS? asked the *Prole*. HOW MANY LIFETIMES WILL YOU HAVE? inquired the *Radar*. "Science, not content to baffle the statesmen of the world with the H-bomb, now confronts us with the greatest human problem of all time," it announced. "Out of the laboratories comes the promise of a new age for all mankind—a new age that, for some, has already begun—with the discovery of the Antigerone. How will the Antigerone affect *you*?" And so on, to end with a paragraph demanding an immediate government statement regarding the position of old-age pensioners in the new circumstances.

The Antigerone [said the *Prole*] is without doubt the greatest advance in medical science since penicillin. It is another triumph of British brains, initiative, and know-how. It offers you longer life in your prime; this is something that is going to affect all our lives. It is likely to affect the age of marriage. With a longer life before them, girls will no longer have the same incentive to teen-age marriage. Families are likely to be larger in the future, and more extensive, too. Many of us will be able to hold our great-great-grandchildren in our arms, perhaps even *their* children. A woman will no longer be considered to be approaching middle age at forty, and this is certain to have a great effect on fashions. . . .

Diana, skipping through the columns with a rueful smile, was interrupted by her telephone bell.

"Oh, Miss Brackley, Sarah here," said Miss Tallwyn's voice, a little breathless. "Have you got the Home Service on?"

"No," said Diana. "I was looking at the papers. We're on our way, Sarah."

"Well, I think you ought to listen to it, Miss Brackley," said Miss Tallwyn, and there was a click as she hung up.

Diana pressed the radio key. A voice swelled in, saying: ". . . moving out of its own province, committing an act of aggression in realms which are the administrative territory of Almighty God. To the other sins of science, which are many, are now added those of pride, and arrogant opposition to the expressed will of God. Let me read you the passage again: the ninetieth psalm: 'The days of our age are three score years and ten; and though men be so strong that they come to fourscore years: yet is their strength then but labor and sorrow; so soon passeth it away, and we are gone.'

"*That* is the law of God, for it is the law of the form He gave us. Our end, no less than our beginning, is a part of His pattern for our lives. 'The days of man are but as grass: for he flourisheth as a flower of the field,' says the one hundred and third psalm. Mark that: 'as a flower of the field'; *not* as the flower of some scientist's horticultural meddling.

"Now science, in its impious vanity, challenges the designs of the Architect of the Universe. It sets itself up against God's plan for man, and says it can do better. It proposes itself as a new golden calf, in the place of God. It sins as the Children of Israel had sinned when it was written of them: 'Thus were they defiled with their own words, and went a-whoring with their own inventions.'

"Even the crimes and sins of the physicists become almost venial before the effrontery of men who have so lost God in their souls that they have the presumption to challenge His dispensation. This satanic temptation now dangled before us will be rejected by all who fear God and respect His laws, and it is the duty of such right-minded men to see to it that the weaker-willed among us are protected from their folly. It is unthinkable that the laws of this Christian land should countenance this flagrant attack upon the nature of man as he was created by God...."

Diana listened thoughtfully to the end. Almost immediately the hymn following the address had started, the telephone rang again. She switched off the wireless.

"Oh hullo, Miss Brackley. Did you hear it?" said Miss Tallwyn.

"Indeed I did, Sarah. Good stirring stuff. Makes one wonder whether healing the sick, and traveling faster than one can on foot, are sinful interferences with the nature of man, too, doesn't it? Anyway, I don't imagine anyone's going to be able to smother it now. Thank you for telling me. Don't ring again, Sarah, I'm going out. I don't suppose there'll be anything more until tomorrow's papers."

———

Diana's Rolls pulled up before Darr House rather in the manner of a large yacht losing way. Amid her own preoccupations Diana had forgotten the trouble there, and she looked at the family-wing with dismayed recollection. Much of the interior débris had already been cleared out of the shell, and dumps of builders' materials in the side garden showed that work was already in hand, but certainly no part of what remained was habitable. She restarted the car, and drove toward the car-park. There was only one other car there, with its bonnet open while a buxom, up-ended young woman peered at the engine. With no more sound than a crunch of gravel Diana came to rest beside her. The young woman looked up startled, and goggled at the Rolls. Diana inquired for Dr. Saxover.

"He's moved into the coach-house flats *pro tem*.," said the girl. "I think he's in there now. Gosh, what a car!" she added with simple envy, as she watched Diana get out. She looked a little harder. "I say, didn't I see your picture in the *Sunday Judge* this morning? You *are* Miss Brackley, aren't you?"

"I am," Diana admitted, with a slight frown. "But I'd be extremely grateful if you'd keep it under your hat. I'd rather not have it known I've been here—I think Dr. Saxover would say the same."

"All right," agreed the girl. "It's no business of mine. But please do tell me one thing: this antigerone stuff the paper talked about, is it—well, is it what they're saying?"

"I've not seen just what the *Judge* is saying," Diana told her, "but I expect they've got it roughly right."

The girl looked at her somberly for a moment. She shook her head.

"In that case I think I'd rather be in my shoes than yours—in spite of the Rolls. But good luck. You'll find Dr. Saxover in Number Four flat."

Diana walked across to the yard, climbed a familiar staircase, and knocked on the door at the top.

Francis opened it, and stared at his visitor.

"Good heavens, Diana! What are you doing here! Come in."

She stepped into the sitting-room. There were half-a-dozen Sunday papers lying about untidily. The room looked smaller than her memory of it, and less ascetic.

"I used to have it all white and clean. I liked that rather better,

I think. It was my flat once upon a time, you know, Francis," she told him. But he was not listening.

"My dear," he said, "it isn't that I'm not glad to see you, but we've been so careful not to reveal any link—and now, just at this time . . . You'll have seen today's papers, of course. It really wasn't wise, Diana. Did anyone see you?"

She told him of the girl in the car-park, and of warning her. He looked concerned.

"I'd better go and see her, and make sure she understands," he said. "Excuse me a moment."

Diana, left alone, drifted across to the window which had been knocked through the old back wall of the coach-house to look across the orchard. She was still standing there, pensive, and unmoving, when he returned.

"She'll be all right, I think," he said. "Good girl, a chemist, and a worker. She's like you used to be; thinks of Darr as a place where we do things, not as a marriage bureau."

"You think that's how I used to be?" Diana said.

"Why, of course, you were one of the steadiest workers"—then something in her tone struck him, and he broke off to glance at her. "What do you mean?"

"Little enough now. It's all long ago, isn't it?" she said. She turned to look out into the orchard again, then at the door which led to the little bedroom. "It's queer," she said, "I ought to hate Darr, but instead, I'm fond of it. I have never been as unhappy as I was here. In there," she nodded toward the door, "is where I used to cry myself to sleep."

"My dear, I'd no idea. I always thought— But why? Or is that a trespassing question? You were very young."

"Yes. I was very young. It is very painful for the young to see their world take on a tarnish. It takes some of them a long time to understand that tarnish is superficial; that it affects appearance, but, if there is nothing worse, the values can remain."

"I was never good at talking in metaphor," Francis observed.

"I know that, Francis. But I was never good at undressing my emotions. The emotions of the young are painfully impatient. They crave shop-finish perfection, and they are not quite human until their charity count has been increased. So let's leave it, shall we?"

"Very well," Francis agreed. "It can scarcely be what brought you here."

"Oddly enough, in a way it is. But the thing that brought me here *now* is the likelihood that I shall not have much chance to come later. I look like being very busy in the immediate future."

"You do, indeed. In fact, I would say 'busy' is a restrained word to apply to the results of kicking a hornets' nest."

"You still think it is a pretty cheap and vulgar way to do it, don't you, Francis?"

"It isn't a way that would ever be likely to commend itself to me, I admit. Are you satisfied with this, yourself?" He waved a hand toward the crumpled newspapers.

"On the whole, and as a beginning, yes," Diana told him. "I have built up my corps—my living examples. The next step is to get it across to the mass of the people before it can be hushed up, and if the approach is vulgar and stupid, well, that's the editor's opinion of his readers."

"Curiously," said Francis, "he seems in almost all cases to assume: A—that all his readers are women, and B—that they alone are going to be the beneficiaries."

Diana nodded.

"I imagine that is due partly to my launching the whole thing off from Nefertiti, partly to practical psychology—and, quite a bit, to caution: you can, if necessary, brush off an article slanted at women more easily than one that purported to give reliable news to men. And the psychology happens to be right, too. The appeal is more immediate."

"If you're suggesting that women are anxious to live longer, but men don't much care, I'm going to disagree thoroughly," Francis objected. "I don't think they like dying any more than women do, oddly enough."

"Of course not," Diana said patiently, "but they don't feel about it the same way. A man may fear death just as much, but in general he doesn't *resent* age and death quite as women do. It's as if a woman lives—well, on more intimate terms with life; gets to know it more closely, if you understand me. And it seems to me, too, that a man is not so constantly haunted by thoughts of time and age as a woman is. Generalizations, of course, but averagely valid, I think. I'd not be surprised to find a connection between that and her greater susceptibility to mysticism, and a religion that promises a hereafter. At any rate, this factor of *resentment* of age and death is strong. So, therefore, is the disposition to grasp any weapon against them.

"That suits my purpose well. I have my corps of women who will fight for their right to use an antigerone. It is now announced to millions more women who will demand it, and any attempt to withhold it will provoke a useful, incensing element of sugges-tion that 'they'—a male government—are trying to oppress women by denying them longer lives. It may not be logical, but I don't think logic is going to count a lot. So that is why I say 'yes,'" Diana concluded.

Francis said, unhappily:

"I can't recall a particular fable that applies exactly, but I'm sure there must be one in which someone showed the population a delicious, mouth-watering cake, munched one slice of it, and then told them he was sorry everybody couldn't have some, but unfortunately there wasn't enough to go round; and then, of course, the crowd tore him to bits."

"But they still wanted the cake," said Diana, "so they marched to the palace, and threw stones at the windows until the King came out on the balcony and promised that he would nationalize all the cooks in the kingdom, and ensure a regular ration of cake for everyone."

"Which did not, however, put the original cake-maker together again," added Francis. He turned a troubled face toward her.

"You've determined to go your own way, my dear. Nothing can stop it now. But do be careful, do be careful. . . . I wonder if, after all, I ought not . . ."

"No," said Diana, "not yet, Francis. You were right before. The opposition hasn't organized yet. Wait a while till we see how it goes in the field. If it doesn't look too good, then you can bring your scientific guns to bear from the heights."

Francis frowned.

"I'm not sure what your intentions are, Diana. Do you see yourself marching at the head of a monstrous regiment of women? Addressing mass rallies? Or perhaps the spirit of your militant great-aunt is tempting you to see yourself sitting on the Front Bench, with your feet on the table? Is it power you want?"

Again Diana shook her head.

"You're confusing the means with the end, Francis. I don't want to *lead* all these women. I'm just making use of them—deceiving them, if you care to say so. The idea of a longer life has an immense superficial appeal to them. Most of them have no notion of what it is really going to *mean* to them. They don't see yet that it will make them grow up—that they simply won't be able to go on for two hundred years leading the nugatory piffling sort of lives that most women do lead; nobody could stand it. . . .

"They think I'm just offering them more of the *same* life. I'm not. I'm cheating them.

"All my life I've been watching potentially brilliant women let their brains, and their talents, rot away. I could weep for the waste of it; for what they might have been, and might have done . . . But give them two hundred, three hundred years, and they'll either have to employ those talents to keep themselves sane—or commit suicide out of boredom.

"And it applies to men almost as much. I doubt if the brilliant ones can develop their full potentialities in a mere seventy years. The clever moneymakers will grow tired of just making money for themselves after sixty or seventy years of it, and turn their cleverness to something more useful. It will become worthwhile. There will be time—time to do really *great* things at last. . . .

"You're wrong if you think I want power, Francis. All I want to do is see that *homo diuturnus* gets born somehow. I don't care how inconvenient he is, how different; he *must* have his chance. If it takes a caesarian to give him a start, it doesn't matter. If the surgeons won't help, then I'll be head midwife, and do it myself. The *only* advance in millions of years, Francis! It *shan't* be crushed—it *shall not,* whatever it costs!"

"We've got beyond that now, Diana. Even if it were to be suppressed now, it would be rediscovered and launched again before very long. You've done the job already. There's no need for you to run into personal danger."

"We're back to our basic difference, Francis. You think it can make its own way: I think of the opposition it is going to meet. Why only this morning I heard a sermon on the wireless . . ." She gave him the gist of it. "It's the institutions, fighting for their lives, that I'm afraid of," she added. "They might delay it for a century, or more."

"You'll be risking a lot—two hundred and fifty years of your life," Francis told her.

"Not worthy of you, Francis," she said, shaking her head. "Since when did anyone take to calculating risks in terms of the number of years he might possibly live? If that is going to be a by-product, we might do better to suppress lichenin ourselves. But I don't think it is."

Francis interlocked his fingers, and stared down at them.

"Diana, in the years since I started Darr many people have worked here, hundreds by now. They have come, and gone. Most of them have left no memories at all. Others one has never forgotten. Some were self-sufficient; others one felt a—a responsibility for. Of course, one feels a responsibility for everyone here, but toward most it is a duty; for a few it is more personal—on a different level. And once one feels that kind of responsibility it doesn't just stop because it is no longer direct; it lingers on, quiescent perhaps until something arouses it, irrational, perhaps, too, but nevertheless it is there. It is as if with just a few people one has been an influence, perhaps unintentionally, which has set them on a particular course, and has thereby acquired at least a partial responsibility for what happens further along. I am feeling that now."

Diana looked down at her toes, considering.

"I don't see why," she said. "Of course, if you had known that I knew anything about lichenin, it could well be so. But you didn't."

"I didn't," he agreed. "So it was not anything consciously to do with that. It was to do with yourself; something that seemed to have happened to you while you were here. I did not know what it was, but I felt it."

"You've not *done* much about it all this time, have you?" said Diana.

"Anyone making the success you have wasn't in much need of help or advice," he pointed out.

"But you think I am now?"

"I am only advising caution as regards your personal safety."

"For which you take it upon yourself, after all this time, to feel some responsibility," Diana remarked, brusquely.

Francis shook his head.

"I am sorry if you regard it as interference. I thought you might understand."

Diana raised her eyes and studied his face.

"I understand," she said, with sudden bitterness. "I understand very well. You are a father feeling responsible concern for his daughter." Her mouth trembled. "Damn, damn you, Francis, damn you! Oh God, I knew I ought to have kept away from here!"

She got up, and walked back to the window. Francis looked at her back. The lines above his brows, and the furrow between them, grew deeper. At length he said,

"I was so much older than you."

"As if that mattered," Diana said, without turning. "As if that *ever* mattered!"

"Old enough to be your father . . ."

" 'Was,' you said. Even though you *were*—for what it mattered—are you now? Don't you understand, Francis? Between us, we've changed even that. How much older than I are you now?"

He went on looking at her back, but with a new, rather bewildered, expression in his eyes.

"I don't know," he said slowly, and paused. "Diana—" he began.

"No!" Diana burst out. She turned. "No, Francis, no! I *won't* let you use that. I—I—"

She broke off, and fled into the inner room.

12

The Sunday papers had broken the dam. On Monday there were headlines:

STILL GLAMOROUS AT EIGHTY? (*Mirror*)
BACK SEAT FOR TEENAGERS? (*Sketch*)
STAND BACK FOR THE OLD FOLK (*Mail*)
PRIORITY FOR HOME AND PEOPLE (*Express*)
ANTIGERONE SETS MORAL PROBLEMS (*News Chronicle*)
NO PRIVILEGE FOR WEALTH (*Trumpeter*)
A NEW APPROACH TO AGE (*Guardian*)

Almost alone, *The Times* appeared to be giving the matter further consideration before pronouncing judgment.

For no particular reason, save that it was to hand, Diana picked up the *Trumpeter* first, and turned to its leader:

It is no less than a national scandal that the Tories should have permitted the greatest discovery of the age to be developed by private enterprise and exploited at rates beyond the reach of any but the idle rich. The idea that those who can afford to pay shall live longer than those who cannot is an outrage upon the people of a democracy, and on the whole conception of the Welfare State. The *Trumpeter* demands in the name of the people that the government shall nationalize the Antigerone forthwith. It must not remain the privilege of the few a moment longer. We call for fair shares for all. Stocks of the Antigerone must be impounded, treatment centres arranged at hospitals, and the public issued with cards entitling them to free treatment under the National Health Act. Share and share alike must be the watchword. And it is to the families of the workers who produce the wealth of this country that priority must be given. . . .

And the *Mail:*

Our first concern is naturally with the old folks. They must have the priority which will give them a few more years of life. It would be an indelible blot upon this country's honour if the young were permitted to seize this new wonder-drug for themselves while the aged must die the sooner for lack of it. A strict order of priorities beginning with the elderly, and entirely free from the influence of wealth or position, should be drawn up at once. . . .

And the *Telegraph:*

Neither the principle of "first come, first served," nor subservience to clamour from organized sections of the community will give adequate guidance in the handling of the latest scientific marvel which, if first reports are confirmed, has just swum into our ken. It must, of course, be made available to all. Rome, however, was not built in a day, and the problem of distribution in a way that will best serve the national interest until supply can be made to catch up with demand requires serious consideration. There can be little doubt that the fortunes of the nation depend to a large extent upon the wisdom and experience of those who direct our economic policies and steer our great industries. It is their capacity to take the long view which has, as a general rule, raised them to their present positions, but even that ability must be to some extent controlled by the knowledge that, often enough, they will not be alive to see its fruits. If, however, their expectation of life were to be extended . . .

And the *Mirror:*

"What?" women all over the country are asking themselves today, "What will it feel like to be not only young in heart at sixty, or seventy, but still young in face and figure, too?"

Well, first, it is going to mean many years in which you can face your mirror with confidence, and without that question nagging at the back of your mind: "Am I losing his love as I lose my looks?"

And, too, it will mean more confidence. How often have you said to yourself: "If I had only known what I know now when I was younger"? Well, in the future that the Antigerone holds for us, you won't need to say that any more; you will have youth *plus* experience, an appeal which is simple and sophisticated at the same time. . . .

The *Gazette:*

A Longer life for YOU—FREE! . . .

Six fortunate readers of the *Gazette* will be among the first to move into the new age. You could be one of those who will receive the latest Antigerone treatment absolutely without charge. . . . All you have to do is to arrange the following twelve benefits of living a longer life in what you feel is their order of importance. . . .

Diana skimmed through the rest of the papers, and pondered them for some minutes. Then she lifted the phone and dialed.

"Good morning, Sarah," she said.

"Good morning, Miss Brackley. It's a good thing you used the private line. The switchboard's been jammed ever since it opened. Poor Violet's going mad down there. Every newspaper, every crank in the country, and practically every trade organization, I should think, trying to get you at once."

"Tell her to instruct the exchange to accept no more calls," said Diana. "Who is on duty in the hall?"

"Hickson, I think."

"Right. Well, tell Hickson to close the doors, and to let in no one except clients with appointments, or members of the staff. He can get someone to help him if he likes, and if a crowd collects outside he's to ring the police. Put some of the drivers and packers on the doors from the loading-bay, and the back entrance. Overtime rates."

"Very well, Miss Brackley."

"And, Sarah, will you fetch Miss Brendon to the phone."

Presently Miss Brendon's voice spoke.

"Oh, Lucy," said Diana, "I've been looking at the papers. They're all 'angled' one way or another. What I want to know is what people are *really* thinking and saying about it. I want you to select five or six intelligent girls on the staff, and put them on the job. You're all to go out into cafés, pubs, espressos, cocktail-bars, laundrettes, if you like, anywhere where people talk, and see what they're really making of it. Arrange between yourselves to get as good a cross-section as you can. Get back about four-thirty to turn in a report. Don't choose anyone who's likely to drink too much. I'll arrange for you to draw four pounds each for expenses from Miss Trafford. Got all that?"

"Yes, Miss Brackley."

"Good. Go ahead then, and get them out as soon as you can. Tell Miss Tallwyn to put me onto Miss Trafford, will you?"

She fixed up several financial matters with Miss Trafford, and then spoke to Miss Tallwyn again.

"I think perhaps I'd better keep away today, Sarah."

"I'm quite sure you had," approved Miss Tallwyn. "Hickson says there are already half-a-dozen people in the hall refusing to leave until they see you. I think a sort of siege is going to set in. It's going to be difficult at lunch time."

"See if you can't arrange for the staff to get in and out through next door's premises. I don't want them to be sent home because if any clients do manage to get to us they must be made to feel confident that all is well with us, whatever is being said outside. As far as possible, things should go on as usual."

"Yes-s-s," said Miss Tallwyn doubtfully. "I'll do my best."

"I'm relying on you, Sarah. If you need me you'll be able to get me here, on the private number."

"I expect they'll try to reach you at the flat, Miss Brackley."

"Don't worry, Sarah. We have two very large, well-tipped commissionaires. Good luck at your end."

"I hope so, I'm sure," said Miss Tallwyn.

——

"It's not ethical," complained the Managing Director.

He looked round the group sitting in Appeal Arts Limited's usual morning conference.

"Four times I've tackled that woman on opening an account with us, and every time the answer was the same: she did not intend to go in for big stuff, the mass-market did not interest her, she depended on personal recommendation. I said she'd be bound to want to expand one day, and we were in an excellent position to plan a campaign for her; in the meantime we had excellent personal-recommendation networks on various levels, and I offered her a trial of the top grade at a nominal figure. But no thank you, said she; got all the custom she was equipped to handle, said she. I gave her all the usual expand-or-die line, but still no. And now look at this! Who's got hold of her? Who's handling her account—hell, handling, did I say? Just look at today's papers. All unpaid stuff, too!"

"Well, whoever's doing it has dropped her right in the—er—mud, anyway," said the Accounts Manager. "It hasn't the earmarks of anyone I know. What a shambles! Amateur, I'd say!"

"We'd better find him and sign him up," somebody suggested. "He's no slouch at putting it over, you've got to admit."

The Managing Director snorted.

"The object of this agency is to promote its clients' interests, not to wreck 'em and make their names stink. Publicity *can* be notoriety, but only so far; and this is a lot further," he said, coldly. "Whoever's done this is a menace to the entire profession. It could shake the whole faith of the public in the integrity of advertising. Instilling hope and faith is one thing; claiming bloody miracles is quite another."

The youngest member of the group cleared his throat diffidently. He was not long down from Oxford, and had been with the firm for little more than a year, but he was the Managing Director's nephew, and faces turned to him attentively.

"I was wondering—" he began. "Well, I mean, we all seem to be taking it for granted that all this is entirely phony. After all, practically every newspaper this morning..." He let it trail away, discouraged by their expressions. "Only an idea . . ." he concluded weakly.

The Managing Director shook his head tolerantly.

"Can't expect to pick up all the angles in a few months, Stephen, you know. It's clever, I'll grant that, but it's the kind of cleverness that blows itself up. I don't care who put it across; it's not *ethical*."

—

Telegram to the Home Secretary:

Sir: At a special emergency meeting of the General Council of The Brotherhood of British Morticians held today the following resolution was passed unanimously: That this Council shall convey to the Government the grave concern of the Members of the Brotherhood regarding the drug Antigerone. Use of this drug, if permitted, could not fail to cause a falling off in the demand for the services of this profession, leading to a serious degree of unemployment among its Members. The Brotherhood earnestly urges that steps should be put in hand immediately to render the manufacture and/or administration of the Antigerone an illegal operation.

—

"I—er—well, I want your opinion of my age, doctor."

"Madam, I am not here to flatter my patients, nor to play guessing games with them. I suggest that if you have no copy of your birth certificate, you apply to Somerset House for one."

"But there could have been a muddle. I mean, there *are* muddles, aren't there? It might not be really *my* birth certificate, or someone *could* have made a mistake in the entry, couldn't they?"

"They *could,* but it is most improbable."

"All the same, doctor, I'd like to be sure. If you could—?"

"If this *is* some sort of game, madam, I am not a player."

"Well, really, doctor—"

"I have been in practice now for thirty-five years, madam. And in all that time not one of my patients who wasn't senile has been in honest doubt about his, or her, age. Now, this morning *two* ladies come to me requiring to be told how old they are. It's preposterous, madam."

"But—well, I mean, coincidences—"

"Besides, it's impossible. The best I could do would be simply an approximation. Scarcely better than a nonmedical guess."

"Is that what you gave the other lady, doctor?"

"I—er—yes, a *rough* approximation."

"Surely, then, you won't refuse to give me just a rough approximation, too, will you, doctor? I mean, it's rather important to me. . . ."

—

"Three coffees, please, Chrissie—I say, chaps, this is getting a bit grim, isn't it? People were saying over the weekend that things would steady up again today. By Saturday morning quite a lot of types were wondering why they'd got into such a flap on Friday."

"Oh, there was a sort of staunch air at the opening. It lasted about ten minutes, then they started to get panicky again. Prices fluttering down like autumn leaves."

"But—oh, thanks, Chrissie . . . That's a-girl. No, Chrissie, if you hit me I shall complain to the Lord Mayor, and he'll put you in the stocks—where was I?"

"You were saying 'but.'"

"Oh, was I? I wonder why? Well, anyway, if there's anything in this Antigerone thing, why doesn't somebody confirm, or deny it, officially? Then we'd know where we stand."

"Haven't you seen a paper today?"

"*The* paper didn't have a thing about it."

"Well, old boy, some *other* Top Persons have highstepping wives who go to Nefertiti, and the furphy round the House is that *they* believe in the thing so solidly that they've convinced their husbands, and that's what's really at the back of it."

"Now look, you two, sober up a minute. This is serious. I think Bill's furphy's right. Oh, maybe it's not so sensational as it sounds, but if there'd been *nothing* in it, it would have been blown wide open by now. This thing has already played hell with the market. If it goes much further I'd not be surprised if the House stops dealings, pending some official statement from somewhere."

"Can it?"

"Why on earth shouldn't it if it wants to, in members' interests? Anyway, I'm betting on this Antigerone being the genuine article—damn it, it'd never have got this far if it weren't."

"So what?"

"So now's the time to buy—everything's way down, isn't it?"

"Buy what, for goodness' sake?"

"All right, but keep it under your hats. Stores."

"Stores!"

"Keep your voice down, you clot, old man. Now, look here, it's obvious really. Did you know that seventy-five percent of the women's clothing sold in this country is bought by women aged seventeen to twenty-five?"

"Is it really? Sounds sort of unfair, but I don't see—"

"It is. Now then, that means that even if this Antigerone isn't all it's cracked up to be—say it only doubles the expectation of life—there are going to be twice as many women sort of thinking they're between seventeen and twenty-five as there are now, so they are going to buy twice as much clothing, aren't they?"

"Er—aren't they *all* going to need twice as much clothing, anyway?"

"All the better. And of course if the Antigerone factor is really three, better still, but even one hundred percent increase in turnover's no sneeze. Go for the big drapers, and you can't fail."

"Yes, but I still don't quite see what seventy-five percent has to do—"

"Never mind. You keep thinking it over, old boy. I'm off to put my lolly in the lingerie...."

—

Telegram: The Prime Minister from Secretary, Sabbath Preservation Society:

The days of our age are threescore years and ten ...

—

"Spiller! Spiller! Where are you?"

"Here, Sir John."

"About time, too. Spiller, you know about this Antigerone thing?"

"Only from certain references in the papers, Sir John."

"What do you think of it?"

"I really can't say, Sir John."

"Been talking to m' wife about it. She believes in it absolutely. Been going to this Nefertiti place for years. Inclined to agree with her. Looks scarcely a day older than when we were married, eh?"

"Lady Catterham preserves her looks wonderfully, Sir John."

"God damn it, man. Don't make her sound like a dowager. Look at that photograph. Taken nine years ago. And she looks just as young, and just as pretty now as she did then. Not a day over twenty-two."

"Quite so, Sir John."

"Either it's uncanny, or there's something in this thing."

"As you say, Sir John."

"I want you to get onto the woman who runs the place—a Miss Brackley. Fix up for a course of treatment right away. No delays. If she gets sticky over bookings offer her twenty-five percent above the usual fee, for quick service."

"But, Sir John, I understood that Lady Catterham already—"

"Oh, for God's sake! Spiller, this isn't for m' wife, it's for *me*."

"Oh—er—yes. I see. Very good, Sir John."

———

"Henry, I see there's a Question down for tomorrow, on this Antigerone business. Have we any more details yet?"

"Not yet, I'm afraid, sir. Nothing reliable, that is."

"Well, do put a jerk into them, there's a good fellow. We don't want the Minister having kittens again, do we?"

"Indeed, not, sir."

"Henry, what is your own unofficial opinion on this?"

"Well, sir. My wife happens to know several ladies who are Nefertiti clients. None of them seems to have any doubt at all that it's the genuine thing. One has to make allowances for exaggeration in some of the newspaper reports, of course, but, on the evidence so far, I'm inclined to believe it can be done—I mean *is being* done."

"I was rather afraid you'd say that, Henry. I don't like it, my boy. Don't like it at all. If the claims are true—or only half-true—the effects are going to be—er—er—"

"Apocalyptic, sir?"

"Thank you, Henry. *Le mot juste,* I fear."

—

"It's just a case of being prepared, Inspector. By the way things are building up it looks as if we're bound to have to pull her in sooner or later—even if it's only for her own protection. I can smell real trouble. You say dangerous drugs is no good?"

"The Superintendent and I have talked that over, sir. We've no evidence of the use of any known drug, and the trouble is that a thing isn't a dangerous drug until it's scheduled as such."

"Suspected possession of?"

"Risky, sir. I'm sure we'd not find anything within the Act."

"Well, you can always pin something on 'em if you really want to. What about vagrancy?"

"Vagrancy, sir?"

"She's been telling 'em they're going to live two hundred years. That's telling fortunes, isn't it? So it makes her a rogue or a vagabond, within the meaning of the Vagrancy Act."

"I'd scarcely think so, sir. She's not actually been foretelling. As I see it, she simply claims to have something that increases the *expectation* of life."

"That could be fraud, nevertheless."

"It *could,* sir. But that's the real question—*is* it? Nobody seems to know."

"Well, we can't wait two hundred years to find out, can we? Seems to me the best thing we can do is to make out a warrant on conduct calculated to lead to a breach of the peace, and hold it till we need it."

"I very much doubt if we'd get it granted on the present showing, sir."

"Maybe, Averhouse, maybe. But today's showing isn't going to be the same as tomorrow's, or the next day's. You mark my words. Anyway, get it filled in as far as you can. I've a feeling we may need it granted in a hurry later."

"Yes, sir. I'll do that."

—

QUEEN AND THE ANTI-G

The *Evening Flag* has no doubt that it voices the sentiments of the overwhelming majority of its readers in urging that top priority in sharing the results of the latest triumph of British science must be given to the First Lady in our land . . .

—

"Two pints, guv. . . . So then I tells 'er straight. I says: 'Look 'ere, my girl,' I says. 'Natcheral's natcheral, and this 'ere ain't. Did your ma tick about not livin' two 'undred years? Did my ma? Naow—and never no more you didn't ought to, neither. 'S not natcheral'— Thanks, guv. 'Ere's 'ow."

"'S right, Bill. 'S *un*bloodynatcheral. Wot she say to that?"

"She tosses 'er 'ead an' says, 'Come to that, our mas didn't 'ave no flippin' telly, neither.' 'I'm not arguing,' I says to 'er, 'I'm just tellin' yer. I know what you're after. You'd like it so you was still rockin' and rollin' in Bikinis an' such when I was safely screwed dahn. Well, you ain't goin' to 'ave it that way, an' that's flat. When they talk about "till death do us part," they don't mean no 'ankypanky about one livin' three times as long as t'other. So you can put this 'ere anti-wotsit right out of your 'ead, 's far as you're concerned. An' if I ever do catch you up to any o' that lark, my girl, I'll bash yer—can't say I 'aven't given yer fair warnin'. 'T'aint natcheral.' Oh, told 'er straight, I did."

"She'd not like that?"

"Naow. Starts snivelin', she does, sayin' as it's not fair, an' as 'ow she's got a right to live as long as she can. 'All right, then,' I says, 'you try it, an' see what 'appens to yer.'

—

"So then she turns the taps on some more, till I yells at 'er to stow it, an' she goes back to snivelin', like. Arter a bit she says: 'I got a right to, if I want to.' So I gives 'er a look. 'An' you got a right to, too,' she says, 'but you don't have no right to say as I can't.' 'That's as maybe,' I tells 'er, 'just you try it an' see.' Then, in a bit, she lays orf of 'er snivelin' an' looks at me kind of steadylike. 'Bill,' she says, 's'pose you was to 'ave this 'ere antithing, too? 'T'ud be the same for both, then, so 't'ud be right.' I looks at 'er. 'See 'ere,' I says, 'two unnatcherals doesn't make a natcheral. Never did. An' wot about me 'avin' to put up with two 'undred flippin' years o' your flippin' tongue? All *right*, says you! Cor strike me flamin' pink! Stone that for a lark!'"

—

"Bert, oh Bert, put it onto the BBC, will you? There's a dear. They got that woman on that tells you what you got to do to live two hundred years. Not that I'm all that keen to live that long. There's times when I know what it *feels* like, already. But it might be nice to know how...."

"Good evening, ladies and gentlemen. Welcome to another program in our Newsmaker series. Our Newsmaker this week has certainly been in the headlines these last few days ... Miss Diana Brackley ... Miss Brackley is interviewed by Rupert Pigeon ..."

"Well, Miss Brackley, your announcement last week certainly seems to have created something of a stir."

"One rather expected it would, Mr. Pigeon."

"Just in case some of our viewers happen to have missed seeing the papers lately, do you think you could give us, quite simply, the essence of your announcement?"

"It *is* quite simple. It is that if people wish to live longer lives, the means to do so is now available."

"I see. That's certainly forthright. And you claim that you have developed a form of treatment which will ensure this?"

"I don't think we need loaded questions, Mr. Pigeon."

"I beg your pardon?"

"Do you *claim* to have had breakfast this morning, or did you have breakfast this morning, Mr. Pigeon?"

"Well, I—"

"Exactly, Mr. Pigeon. Tendentious, is it not?"

"Er—your announcement clai— I mean, you announced that a number of people have already had treatment from you which will have this effect."

"I did."

"How many people, roughly?"

"Several hundred people."

"All women?"

"Yes, but that is an effect of circumstances. It is equally effective with men."

"And how long are these people going to live?"

"I couldn't possibly tell you, Mr. Pigeon. How long are you going to live?"

"But I understood that you claimed— I mean, said—"

"What I said was that their average expectation of life had been increased, and that if the treatment were continued they could expect to double the normal expectation, or to treble it, according to the quality of the treatment given. That is quite different from saying how long anyone is going to live. For one thing, when you double the expectation of life, you also double the chances of a fatal accident, and it appears likely that you more than double susceptibility to illness."

"Then someone whose expectation has been trebled doesn't stand as good a chance of realizing it as she would of realizing her normally expected age?"

"No."

"But, barring accidents and serious illness, she *could* live to see her two hundredth birthday?"

"Yes."

"Well now, Miss Brackley, it has been stated by more than one newspaper that none of these people you have been treating with your Antigerone—is that right?"

"Antigerone, yes."

"That none of them was aware that she was having this treatment until you made your announcement a few days ago?"

"I think one or two may have guessed."

"You mean you don't deny it?"

"Why should I want to deny it?"

"Well, I should have thought it was a rather grave charge to make. Here are all these people coming along and putting themselves in your hands in good faith, and there you are treating them with this Antigerone which is going to make them live two hundred years, without even telling them about it. It seems to me that it could be a pretty serious matter."

"It is. If one is facing the prospect of two hundred years of—"

"I was referring to the—well, the element of deception that is implied in the statements."

"Deception? What do you mean? There was no deception—in fact the very opposite."

"I'm afraid I don't quite—"

"It's quite simple, Mr. Pigeon. I run a business that we are not allowed to name over the air. These ladies came to me as clients and said, in effect, that they wanted their youth and beauty preserved. Well, that's jargon of course; no one can preserve it. But I said I could prolong it for them. They said that was what they meant, really; so that's what I've done. Where is the deception?"

"Well, it is hardly what they must have expected, Miss Brackley."

"You're implying that they expected to be deceived, and that I am guilty of deceiving them by giving them what they asked for instead of the deception they expected. Is that it, Mr. Pigeon? I really can't think you're on very firm ground there. The whole of my trade professes to prolong youth and beauty. I am the one member of it who does what she is asked—who delivers the goods—and you talk about a 'grave charge.' I just don't understand you, Mr. Pigeon."

"You clai—— I mean, your treatment with the Antigerone is always one hundred percent successful and safe?"

"Out of my several hundred clients there has been only one failure. A lady who suffered from a rare, unsuspected allergic condition."

"So you would not say it is infallible?"

"Certainly not. Only that it is well over ninety-nine percent successful."

"Miss Brackley. It has been suggested that if the Antigerone were to be widely used—indeed, if it is used at all—it will have far-reaching effects upon our social system. Would you agree with that?"

"Certainly."

"What sort of effects do you envisage?"

"Can you think of anything that would *not* be affected if we were all to have the opportunity of living two hundred years?"

"I believe that, as yet, Miss Brackley, there has not been any scientific investigation into your clai—— er, into the Antigerone?"

"That is a mistake, Mr. Pigeon. I have, as a biochemist, investigated it very thoroughly."

"I—er—well, shall we say *independent* investigation?"

"Not yet."

"Would you welcome such an investigation?"

"Why should I *welcome* it? I'm perfectly satisfied with the efficacy of the Antigerone."

"Let us say, then, would you object to it?"

"Again, why should I? Frankly, Mr. Pigeon, I don't give a damn. The one thing to be said in favor of an investigation is that it might perhaps lead on to the discovery of other, perhaps preferable, types of Antigerone."

"Miss Brackley. One thing that has been causing a lot of speculation is the nature of the Antigerone."

"It is a chemical substance, possibly one of a class of such substances produced by micro-organisms, that has the property of retarding certain of the metabolic processes, and bears a distant chemical relationship to the antibiotics."

"I see. Could you, perhaps, tell us the source of this substance?"

"I prefer not to disclose it just yet."

"Don't you think, Miss Brackley, that it would—er—inspire more confidence if you could give us some indication?"

"We seem to be rather at cross purposes, Mr. Pigeon. What makes you think I want to 'inspire confidence'? I am not a faith healer, or a politician. The Antigerone exists. It doesn't depend on confidence for its results, any more than castor oil does. Whether people 'believe in it,' as the phrase goes, or don't 'believe in it,' will not have the least effect on its properties. . . ."

"Oh, switch over to the ITV, Bert, there's a dear. She's not going to tell us anything. Might 'uv known it'd turn out to be just a lot of BBC highbrow stuff. That's better. . . ."

—

"Darling . . . You awake?"

"Uh . . ."

"Darling, I've been thinking—about this Antigerone thing . . ."

"Uh?"

"Well, it's going to be a long time, isn't it? Longer than we thought, I mean. Would you call two hundred years for better, or for worse, darling? I—wuh—wuh—wuh—wuh . . . !"

"What on earth are you mumbling about?"

"Mumbling! I like that! I was suffocating. *I* don't think people ought to be *allowed* to wear beards in bed. I—wuh—wuh—wuh . . . !"

. . . .

"But, duckie, you *still* haven't answered my question."

"Oh, for worse. Definitely for worse."

"Oh, darling, you pig!"

"Ought to be three hundred years, at least."

"Unpig . . . Oh, da-a-a-arling . . . !"

—

"This is Radio Moscow.

"Referring to reports in the London papers, the Moscow newspaper *Izvestia* states today:

"The British press announcements of the discovery of a drug that will extend the normal expectation of life does not come as any great surprise to the well-informed citizens of the People's Republics of the U.S.S.R. The Russian people are well acquainted with the pioneer work in this field of the Geriatrics Department of the State Clinic at Komsk under the direction of Hero of Soviet Science Comrade Doctor A. B. Krystanovitch. Scientists in the U.S.S.R. are little impressed by the unproved claims made in London. They point out that this development, based no doubt on the work of A. B. Krystanovitch, is being exploited in England by capitalist interests, and that the claims made can therefore be considered to be exaggerated from motives of private profit.

"Thus there is demonstrated once again, in the work of A. B. Krystanovitch the lead that is constantly being given to the rest of the world by the swift progress of Soviet Science..."

—

"Good evening, Constable."

"Good evening, sir. You all right?"

"A little drunk, Constable. Take no notice. Not incapable, not dish-disorderly. Just a little drunk."

"You'd better be getting home, sir."

"On my way, Constable. Live near here. This is most exceptional—most exceptional."

"Glad to hear it, sir. All the same, if I was you—"

"But you don't know *why* I got drunk, do you? I'll tell you. It's this woman with her anti—anti—well, it's anti-something..."

"Antigerone, sir?"

"That's it. Antigerone. Well, you see, I'm interested in satis—statsisticks. I've been working it out. Once this anti—anti-thing gets going we shall all starve. Less than twenty years, all starve. Very sad. So I got drunk. Very exceptional."

"Well, sir, we shall have to see to it that it doesn't get going, shan't we?"

"No good, Constable. Will to survive's too strong. We shan't be able to stop it. Individual will to survive's part of life-force. 'S all a matter of balance. Too much life-force's self-destructive. Ever think of that, Constable?"

"Can't say I have, sir. Now, hadn't you better get along home. It's gone midnight, you know."

"All right, Constable. On my way. Just wanted to tell you, that's all. All starving in less than twenty years. Very serious state 'f affairs. Don't forget I told you."

"I'll bear it in mind, sir. Good night."

"Good night, Constable."

13

"Where are you?" asked Lady Tewley.

"Out here. Come along, Janet," called Diana's voice.

Janet Tewley stepped to the window.

"Oh, Diana. What an adorable garden, right up here. No one would ever suspect it."

"I love my little garden," Diana said, straightening up, and pulling off her gloves. "I'm glad you managed to get in."

"My dear, without your special permit I'd not have got near. You seem to have a whole corps of Commissionaires to guard you."

"It's necessary, unfortunately," said Diana. "I had to smuggle out in a tradesman's van to get to that broadcast on Monday, *and* send a decoy to the front entrance in my car so that I could get safely back again. I've been a prisoner ever since. Come and sit down. We'll have some coffee while you tell me what's been going on."

"I can't stay long. I'm frantically busy."

"It's going well?"

"The League, you mean? Oh, yes. Lydia Washington has been elected Leader. She's a good choice, ready to work like the devil, and not scared of anybody, or anything. She's got a good nucleus of a Council together already, and she's thoroughly enjoying herself, too."

"So are you, by the look of you, Janet."

"Oh, I am. The only trouble is it doesn't seem to leave much time for sleep. Never mind though, that can come later. But Diana, my dear, I do lift my hat to you. Now we've really looked ourselves over we seem to be wives, or daughters, of half the Establishment. We're married to four Cabinet Ministers, three other Ministers, two Bishops, three Earls, five Viscounts, a dozen blue-chip companies, half-a-dozen Banks, twenty-three members of the Government, eight members of the Opposition, and lots of others. In addition, we have close relations that are not quite marital with a lot of other Influences. So, you see, one way and another, there isn't much we don't know, or can't get to know."

"That's what I want. In the last three days I've had practically nothing but what the newspapers and the BBC have told me. And bits from Sarah, at the office. I gather that the chief trouble has come from the *Trumpeter*?"

"Oh, yes, there was a lovely row there. They found they'd backed the wrong horse from the party point of view on Monday, and the poor editor went out on his neck. The very next day they came out with the Opposition line. Exploitation of the workers. Prospect of three lifetimes spent at the factory bench. Inevitable rise in unemployment. Impossibility of paying adequate pensions even if the age of retirement were raised by a hundred years. Lack of opportunities for promotion. Favoritism of the rich. Favoritism of the intellectuals. Favoritism of all upper administrative and managerial grades. Entrenchment of the Monarch. (That was a bad line to take, and they dropped it quick.) Lack of opportunity for the young. No fresh blood in anything. Rise in prices owing to increased demand by increased population. Breakdown of National Health Service faced by population problems, and so on. Call to all unions to register unanimous massive vote of protest. Hints of general strike action unless use of the Antigerone is made a criminal offense.

"On the way here I passed a wall, somewhere Notting Hill way, scrawled with BAN ANTI-G! ALL OUT ON DEMO. TRAF SQ SUNDAY.

"They'll get an impressive vote, all right. You know the way they reckon the figures. Besides, who wants to be threatened, or sent to Coventry?—No secret ballot; their Chartist ancestors shed blood for that, but they ... Anyway, it won't mean a lot. The wives aren't for the ban, whatever they may tell their men. For one thing there was that gaffe about the Queen; for another, they don't think much of the idea of their husbands voting for shorter lives for *them*."

"And the Church? I heard a sermon on Sunday ..."

"No need to worry. He jumped the gun, and got away in the wrong direction. Cantuar's pro, Ebor's qualified pro, Bath and Wells is pro, in fact, they're all more or less pro, though Llandaff and Newcastle are shaky. After all, being an anti would almost amount to counseling suicide by neglect of opportunity to live, wouldn't it? Though there are some small sects who are taking what they claim to be a fundamentalist line. Rome still seems to be thinking it over—and our communications aren't so good there, for obvious reasons.

"The Stock Exchange got out of hand, and has had to close down for a bit—but I expect you know that.

"On the whole, I think it's not going so badly. Our members are putting in a lot of fifth column work, domestic and social, and it seems as though we may not have to come out with a full-scale New Life Party at all, but we're not counting on that. As I told you, Lydia Washington's getting the organization together and ready, in case we need it.

"We hear the P.M.'s very unhappy indeed, poor man. If he sanctions use of the Anti-G there'll be chaos everywhere, and riots from the Left. If he tries to ban it, there'll be such an outcry and near-revolution that our New Life Party will come towering up almost overnight. At present they're offering four to one in the clubs that he sanctions, on the grounds that it will have to come sooner or later, so why let foreigners get in with it first? The eventual outcome will be a population with greater experience, and therefore greater ability, so we'd gain by being first ourselves."

Diana nodded.

"Well, at least they're beginning to have some realization of what it is going to mean," she said.

"But that's only a part of the poor man's anxieties," Janet Tewley went on. "If he does agree to sanction it, then there'll be the whole question of dealing with China."

"*China!*" Diana exclaimed, in dismay.

"My dear, you don't have to look surprised with me," Janet told her.

"But I *am* surprised," Diana said. Then she recollected Richard's and Zephanie's uncomfortable experience. From Zephanie's account there had been three men there when she had admitted the source of the supply. It could have leaked out from any one of them. "What about China?" she added.

"It is said to be the only source of the particular lichen that yields the Antigerone," Janet said, her eyes on Diana's face.

"I see." Diana's voice and expression were non-committal.

"So once the Chinese find out *why* we want to buy their lichen—well, that will finish that. They'll want it for themselves, and even if they don't, we'd be a long way down on the list of customers."

Diana nodded again.

"It could be more troublesome than that," she said. "Once the Chinese know, the Russians will know. The lichen doesn't come from China proper. It grows in northern Manchuria, close to the

Russian border. If the Russians were to think it valuable enough to be worth grabbing, anything might start."

"Anyway, it looks as if *we* shan't get it," Janet commented, "and in that case what happens? Is there any point in conducting a campaign for the Antigerone at all?"

Diana hesitated.

"I didn't agree that it was the only source," she pointed out.

"All right. Be cautious if you like. I'm just telling you what's being said—that this lichen is imported from China, and is processed to produce the Antigerone for you, at Darr House."

Diana suddenly sat up.

"But that's utterly untrue. I import the lichen, and I have it processed, but it doesn't go anywhere near Darr House. That's a complete fabrication."

"My dear, don't glare. *I* didn't fabricate it."

"No. Of course not, Janet. But of all the sickening, *stupid* things to happen . . . Oh, you wait here a few minutes, Janet. I must think."

Diana went back to the window, and out into the little garden. She stood there, looking out over the tree tops of the park for nearly ten minutes before she returned. Her manner was brisk.

"Janet, I want to broadcast. I don't care what service, but some time on Saturday evening. One of those bits and pieces programs would do, if necessary. Only ten minutes. Five would be enough. I want to tell them *all* about the Antigerone—the questions I wouldn't answer before. Do you think that it could be fixed?"

Janet smiled.

"In the circumstances, *any* hesitation by any of the services seems highly unlikely, my dear. But I don't see how anything you can say is going to alter the position much. At least, not unless you *have* some other source of supply . . . ?"

"Never mind about that now. Just get it fixed up for me, there's a dear. And get it announced—make sure that it's announced."

"Oh, they'll announce it all right. But I don't see—"

"It's all right, Janet. I know what I'm doing. Just do that for me, and then get on with organizing the League. It looks as if it will have to declare itself before long. . . ."

Janet Tewley left a few minutes later. The door had scarcely closed behind her when Diana was on the telephone to her office:

"Oh, Sarah, will you find Miss Brendon, and send her round here. Give her a card to get her in. . . . Yes, it's most important. I can't explain now, but something's happened. We'll have to put everything forward . . . Yes, I think so, but there's not a lot of time. That's why I want her here quickly. . . ."

"Very well, Miss Brackley . . . Oh, by the way, I have a cable here from America. It's addressed to Nefertiti. It says:

"'Hold all deals pending our seven-figure offer Antigerone rights.'

"It's signed: Ben Lindenbaum, President, Pursuit of Happiness Drug Corporation, Inc., Brooklyn, N.Y. Shall I . . . ?"

———

A motor-coach pulled off the road onto the grass verge and put out all its lights. Figures descended one by one, and stood peering about them with eyes not yet accustomed to the starlit dimness. A voice said quietly, but loud enough for them all to hear:

"All set? All got your stuff?"

There were murmurs of assent.

"Okay. Now keep it fixed in your heads. *One* owl hoot means that Jimmy's cut the phone wires—they all go out of the place together, so that'll isolate the whole set-up. Then you wait. If anybody spots you, jump him before he can raise an alarm, and see he'll keep quiet. Now, when you hear *three* owl-hoots close together, you do your stuff—and not before. *Three* owl-hoots, remember. Everybody got that?

"Right then. Watch your step—and watch the way we go. You'll be finding your own way back here—and we'll not be waiting long for stragglers. Come on now...."

14

Diana awoke to the ringing of the telephone beside her bed. She reached for it reluctantly. "Yes?" she said.

The operator's voice told her.

"Good morning, Miss Brackley. Sorry to wake you, but there's a call for you from a Miss Saxover. She's on your list, and says it's important."

Diana came fully awake in a moment.

"Yes. Put her through, please."

"Diana? It's Zephanie."

"Yes. What is it, Zephanie?"

"Oh, Diana. It's Darr again. It's all been burnt—burnt right out this time. Daddy's been taken to hospital and—"

Diana's heart jumped suddenly, and hurt for a moment. She clutched the receiver.

"Oh, Zephie! What's happened to him? What—what—?"

"It's all right, Diana. He's not badly hurt. Not burnt, I mean. He had to jump out of the window, and he's rather shaken up. He was sleeping in the coach-house flats, you know—"

"Yes, yes. But is that all? He's not hurt otherwise?"

"No. Only a few bruises, the hospital says."

"Thank God for that. . . . What happened, Zephie?"

"We're not quite sure. It seems like a raid by quite a lot of people. It happened all over the place at once. One man says he was awake, and didn't hear anything until suddenly there was a noise of breaking glass in all directions. Apparently they threw lighted bottles of something through the windows. Not petrol, he says, something much fiercer. It set off the house, and the flats, and the lab blocks, and some of the staff houses, all at practically the same time.

"The phones wouldn't work, so Austin got out his car to go and fetch help. He ran into a wire stretched across the drive near the lodge. It wrecked the car and blocked the drive, and poor Austin's in hospital, too. He's got a lot of nasty cuts and a broken rib, poor man.

"And dear old Mr. Timpson—you remember old Timmy, the watchman? They found his body in the stable yard. The police say he was coshed. A poor old man like that! Only one blow, thank God. He can't have realized it.

"But it's all gone, Diana. The house, the labs, the stores, everything but a few of the staff houses. There wasn't anything anybody could do. By the time they found out what had happened to Austin it was practically all over.

"Daddy managed to drag himself a bit away from the coachhouse, or he'd have been buried when it collapsed."

"Thank God for that," said Diana. "Have the police any idea who did it?"

"I don't think so. They told Raikes, who has taken charge at Darr for the moment, that they 'had reason to believe' that it was a gang who came from somewhere else, in a lorry. Raikes said that was a masterly bit of deduction."

"Zephie, you're *sure* your father hasn't any real injuries?"

"He's sprained his left wrist a bit, but otherwise we're as sure as we can be until we see the X-rays. What I've been wondering, Diana, is whether it will take him longer to get over it—longer, I mean, than people who don't have you-know-what?"

"I can't tell you, Zephie. The wrist'll take longer to recover, of course, bruises too, and cuts, if there are any. But general shaking, and I suppose a degree of shock, I simply don't know. I shouldn't *think* it would show any noticeable delay. That's what you're thinking of?"

"One doesn't want the doctors to start prying."

"No, of course. We'll have to watch that. You will, I mean. Give him my—my very best wishes."

"I will. By the way, Diana, what's this about you giving another broadcast tomorrow night? Is it true?"

"Yes. How did you hear?"

"They slipped it in among the announcements before the news this morning. It sounded—what *are* you going to tell them?"

"All about it, Zephie. If I don't do it publicly now, I can see them putting me under some kind of subpoena to do it more privately before long. Publicly would be better, I think."

"But nothing about Daddy?"

"You can ask him, but I think you'll find he'll still think his weight will tell more later on—and he's got more than enough trouble on his hands at the moment."

"All right. I'll ask him. And let you know."

"Very well. And don't forget to give him—to tell him I—"

"I won't, Diana. 'Bye."

———

Diana searched through the papers for news of the Darr House disaster. Apparently it had come in too late for even the London editions. But there was plenty of reference to the Antigerone. *The Times* gave it a second leader for the second time, and printed half-a-dozen letters which, though the approaches varied from the drily factual to the verge of superstitious alarm, all conveyed serious anxiety. The *Guardian* appeared to be torn between a liberal respect for any form of new knowledge, and a statistical lament at the consequences of this one. The *Trumpeter* had not changed its mind again, but change had crept into its attitude. Though its call for suppression of the ANTI-G was still firm, the purity of emotional response seemed to have been sullied by a tincture of thought. There was no longer quite the same impression that the party had just received the gift of a brand-new, twelve-cylinder vote-catcher and crowd-rouser.

Indeed, in almost all the popular papers some shift of attitude was perceptible, almost as though word had been going round Fleet Street that the Antigerone had potentialities beyond that of increasing the female readership.

To Diana, the most interesting, and also most gratifying, feature was negative: scarcely anywhere was there a disposition to question the validity of the Antigerone. An omission which, in the circumstances, testified not only to the confidence of Nefertiti's clients, but to the success they must have had in convincing husbands, friends, and widespread acquaintances. That was far better than she had hoped for. She must, she decided, have underestimated the weakening effect wrought by successive scientific marvels upon popular skepticism; so that where she had expected to find the first barricades there was almost no resistance.

Nor was engagement Number Two developing along the lines she had expected. True, the *Trumpeter*, after a false start, had rather taken up a position according to the book, but, so far, at any rate, almost alone. She had envisaged a consolidation of opposing forces—that the clerk, the shop assistant, routine workers of all kinds would discover that the objection of the man at the bench was, this time at least, equally valid in their own circumstances, and hurry to make common cause with him. It puzzled her to decide whether some such consolidation was merely delayed by slow comprehension, or whether she had again overestimated public resistance to discoveries. But, on further consideration, she began to wonder if she had not, certainly as far as the men were concerned, allowed herself to simpify the position too much. She perceived two factors which she had, perhaps, weighed too lightly. One was schizophrenic: resistance to the prospect of a greatly prolonged life of monotonous work was in conflict with the strong personal will to survive at any cost, and had resulted for many in a state of helpless indecision. The other was fatalistic: a feeling that the goings-on of science had got so far beyond ordinary human control, and any new discovery now came so nearly into the category of Act of God, that it was scarcely worth troubling oneself to try to do anything about them.

Anyway, whatever the causes, Diana could perceive that the fight was not going to be quite the free-for-all she had envisaged, but something more like a large-scale tourney, with a large spectatorship whose favor could be swayed to one side or the other.

Considering the situation, she decided that her original strategic plan would be assisted rather than hindered by the development.

Nevertheless, gratifying though an easy victory in Phase One followed by discovery of weaknesses in the enemy forces may be, it plays havoc with a careful timetable. There is an anxious interlude when it is uncertain whether reserves can be brought forward in time to exploit the advantage.

Reading, however, in each newspaper announcements of various prominence that the Saturday night play on the Home Service would be postponed from nine-fifteen to nine-thirty in order to give Miss Diana Brackley an opportunity of making a statement regarding the Antigerone, she was able to feel that the next phase could now begin . . . —

The lift-doors opened, and a small party stepped out into the hall. First, Diana, in a semi–evening dress of pale gray peau-de-soie, long white gloves, an emerald pendant at her throat, and a light, fur-collared wrap about her shoulders. Behind her, Lucy Brendon and Sarah Tallwyn. The former dressed less strikingly, but also with some air of occasion; the latter in a rather severe dress of dark blue which suited her air of being in charge of proceedings. And last, Ottilie, Diana's maid, in attendance to see the party off.

The hall-porter left his desk, and came forward with an air of concern.

"There's quite a bit of a crowd outside, Miss Brackley," he told her. "We could put some chairs in one of the vans, and take you out again that way, if you like?"

Diana glanced through the glass upper panels of the door. The crowd must number nearly a hundred, she judged, predominantly feminine, but with a score or so of men, including two with press cameras. The car, guarded by the under-porter, stood at the curb, beyond.

"We're a little late as it is, Sergeant Trant. I think we'll use the car."

"Very good, Miss." The sergeant crossed the hall to the door, unlocked it, and stepped outside. His gesture to the crowd was quite imperious. After a brief hesitation, it parted reluctantly to leave a narrow lane down the steps and across the pavement.

"Thank goodness we're only temporary royalty," Miss Brendon murmured to Miss Tallwyn. "Fancy having to go through this several times a day."

The sergeant, after a menacing survey of the crowd which dared it to encroach again, held the door wide. The three ladies, with Diana in the lead, stepped forward, leaving Ottilie hovering anxiously in the hall. Across the pavement, the under-porter who had brought the gray Rolls round, and guarded it, had the door open, ready for her. Lucy caught a voice saying: "Forty, they say. Looks like a girl, don't she?"

Diana crossed the broad top step, and started down. The two photographers let off their flashes.

Three loud cracks sounded, fast upon one another.

Diana staggered, and clutched at her left side. The crowd stood frozen. A red mark appeared below Diana's hand. Blood trickled out between her white-gloved fingers. A widening patch of scarlet dyed the pale gray silk. Diana took a half-step back, collapsed, and slithered down the steps . . .

The photographers' flashes blinked again . . .

The under-porter left the car door, and jumped toward her. The sergeant pushed Lucy Brendon aside, and ran down the steps. Diana lay limp, her eyes closed. The two porters made as if to lift her. But a voice said quietly, with authority,

"Don't move her."

The sergeant looked round to see a youngish man wearing horn-rimmed glases, and a well-cut dark suit.

"I am a doctor," he said. "You might do harm. Better send for an ambulance at once."

He bent over Diana, and picked up her hand to feel her pulse.

The sergeant ran back up the steps, but found himself fore-stalled. Ottilie was already at his desk, telephone in hand.

"Ambulance, yes, yes, quick!" she was saying. "That the ambulance? Please come at once to Darlington Mansions—yes, a lady has been shot. . . ."

She hung up.

"Did you get him?" she demanded.

"Who?" asked the sergeant.

"The man who did it," Ottilie said impatiently. "A little man in a raincoat, with a green felt hat. He was on the left," she told him as she made for the door, and ran down the steps to Diana and the doctor.

The sergeant followed, and looked over the crowd. There was no center of commotion. The man must have got away before anyone realized what had happened. The doctor, kneeling beside Diana now, looked up.

"Can't you clear some of these damned people away?" he asked irritably.

The two porters began to push the crowd back and make a wider space.

Diana's eyes opened. Her lips moved. The doctor bent his head closer to catch what she said. Her eyes closed again. He looked up, frowning anxiously.

"That ambulance—" he began.

The sound of its bell interrupted him. It came down the street at speed, and pulled in behind the Rolls. The attendants got out, dragged out a stretcher, and shoved their way through the crowd.

Half a minute later Diana had been loaded aboard. The doctor and Miss Brendon climbed in after her, and the ambulance went clanging on its way.

———

At nine-fifteen the Home Service announcer said:

"We regret to announce that the rearrangement of our programs scheduled for this time will not now take place. Miss Diana Brackley, who was to have spoken about her discovery of the Antigerone, and its significance, at this time, was attacked earlier this evening while on her way to Broadcasting House. Her assailant fired three shots at her. Miss Brackley died in the ambulance on her way to hospital. . . ."

———

On Sunday afternoon the weather cleared, leaving the pavement of Trafalgar Square damp from the morning's drizzle. Contingents from various parts had begun to arrive some time ago, and now, with sandwiches eaten and furled banners leaned against the lions, were beginning to gather expectantly before the north plinth of the column where a white streamer proclaimed in letters of fluorescent red paint:

BAN THE ANTI-G

The contingents of marchers, increased by sympathizers and relatives, formed a good crowd, but not, for a matter of importance and at such a recognized time and place for rallies, a great crowd. Behind and about them strolled the usual London Sunday sightseers, some interested, some curious over anything that might be going on, some seeking company to kill an empty afternoon. Further off, beyond the fountains, the people were closer together again. Most of them were women.

Three or four young men idled about the plinth rearranging wires, seeing that the loudspeaker tripods were stable, tapping the microphone, and reassuring one another with nods. At last there was a stir at the edge of the supporting crowd. A short broad man, with an escort of several waymakers, worked toward the front, smiling and waving to acknowledge greetings as he came. A number of hands helped him up onto the plinth, and he shook hands with several men who awaited him there. At this moment it occurred to one of the young men that all was not yet perfect respecting the technical arrangements, and there was a slight delay while he impressively swathed a handkerchief round the microphone. That done, the speaker stepped forward amid scattered shouts of welcome and a burst of clapping. He beamed at the crowd, gave several more waves of acknowledgment, then he raised his arms in a quelling gesture. His expression shed all traces of amiability, and became grimly portentous, as he waited for the crowd to take his mood. He lowered his arms, paused, then suddenly raised his right hand, pointing at the streamer stretched above his head.

"The Antigerone," he said, "the dirtiest weapon of all the dirty weapons that the Tories have aimed at the workers. The bomb with the selective fall-out—that falls on the workers. The men who live lives of comfort and luxury are happy with the Anti-G— of course they are. For them it means more years—many more years—of that comfort and luxury. But what does it mean to us, the workers, who produce the wealth that buys that comfort and luxury? I'll tell you what it means to us. It means working for *three* lifetimes instead of one. And if you are going to keep on working for three lifetimes, where are your sons going to find work? Yes, and your sons' sons, too. It means two generations, two whole generations of unemployment, two generations on the dole, two generations born to rot in unemployment that will bring down *your* wages. I tell you that never in the history of the whole working-class struggle—"

Up on the north side of the Square a van had stopped opposite the National Gallery. A panel in its side swung open to reveal the trumpets of eight loudpeakers. A contralto voice, heroically enlarged, swept across the crowds.

"Murderers! Cowards! Woman-killers!"

The speaker, taken aback by the blast of sound, hesitated, and lost his thread, but he rallied quickly, and began again:

"Two generations—"

One of the young men resourcefully turned a dial to increase the power. Even so, his apparatus could not contend with the voice from the north, which was continuing:

"It is only people that you kill by murder. Ideas live on. Diana Brackley lies dead, shot for her discoveries. But you can't shoot discoveries dead. . . ."

Almost everyone in the Square had turned to look at the van, and at the policemen running toward it.

"She brought us a gift of life: and her reward is death. But ideas are born of the mind and the spirit, not of a woman's body that can be shot down. . . ."

The policemen had reached the van and were battering at its rear doors, but the Voice went on:

"What do you know of life, you cowards who are so afraid of it that you crush it? What right have you to deny life to us? What right have you to say to us who gave you life, to your mothers, your wives, and your daughters who love life, that they shall die before they must?"

One of the policemen having dragged the driver from his seat, took his place, and began to drive the van away.

"Over," said the contralto voice.

The speaker on the plinth watched the van move off, with relief. He opened his mouth to begin again, but before he could utter a word another stentorian female voice cut in, this time from behind him:

"Don't let your success in shortening one life go to your heads. We're not going to let you shorten all our lives. We've met you before. You are the dolts, the dimwits, the Luddites. And now you carry Luddism to its logical conclusion—don't stop at smashing the machines, smash the inventors, too, and they won't invent any more."

More police were now moving, hot-foot and panting, in a new direction.

"Obstruct, deprive, oppose—and kill. Is that your fine creed? There have been tyrannies where life was held cheap—but none so tyrannous that it would curtail the lives of its whole population."

The police wasted no time trying to get inside the second van. They simply drove it off, and it departed, as had the other, with a valedictory: "Over."

When the voice of the third van came in, from the west side, policemen who had removed their helmets to mop their brows, cursed, replaced the helmets, and started off again.

They had grasped the idea.

Van Number Three had time to deliver only a few sentences before it, too, was driven away.

They were looking out for Number Four, on the east side, and were on it almost before it began. It managed to say no more than "Remember Diana Brackley, martyred by the forces of stupidity, reaction, and self-interest," before it followed the others.

Everybody hopefully scanned the surrounding roads for another vehicle that looked likely to emit a Voice. But no Number Five van manifested itself. The crowd by the column gradually returned its attention to the plinth, though not all its attention, for it was dotted here and there with groups of indignant argument. The speaker set about recapturing his audience, raising his arms again for silence, the arguers were told by their neighbors to stow it. The speaker drew breath, and at that moment there occurred another interruption.

The further crowd, back beyond the fountains, began to chant, uncertainly at first, but with increasing decision and rhythm:

"Murderers . . . ! Cowards . . . ! Woman-killers . . . !"

The new assault brought the speaker's crowds round again, with expressions on its faces that were far from amiable. It hesitated. The speaker himself did his best to call back its attention, but only snatches of his words could get through the swelling chant.

Slowly his crowd made up its mind, and started to move toward the other.

Already, the policemen were sprinting from all directions to put themselves between the two bodies before they could meet, and now the mounted constables rode in, with their horses' hoofs striking sparks from the pavement . . .

—

Monday was a busy day at Bow Street.

—

The funeral took place on Wednesday. After it was over, the great crowd dispersed quietly. The police reinforcements that had stood by unneeded, pinched out their cigarettes, climbed into their vans, and departed, too.

Only the mounds of flowers remained.

But some two hours later many of the faces seen at the funeral were to be seen again in Trafalgar Square. For an hour or more the great open space continued to fill up with a crowd in which women vastly predominated.

Police circulated advising the groups to move along, which they did, only to re-form a moment later.

At about seven o'clock banners started to appear:

THE LEAGUE FOR THE NEW LIFE

and placards bearing simply the initials:

LNL

Young women were hoisted up in the crowd to scatter handfuls of badges, white discs with the letters LNL printed on them in fluorescent orange.

A great four-pole banner with a deep black border and a wreath of flowers at the top of each pole miraculously appeared:

IN MEMORY OF
DIANA BRACKLEY—MURDERED
LIFE WAS HER WORK
DEATH HER REWARD

Elsewhere, several large portraits of Diana rose above the heads of the crowd, and there was one blown-up photograph of her, taken as she lay on the steps.

Signs of marshaling and organization were to be seen. The police stationed groups of men ready to draw a cordon across the top of Whitehall.

The crowd bulged, and began to flow into the roadway on the south side. The traffic there came to a halt. Hastily, the police held up the Whitehall traffic, and formed a line across the road. The crowd rolled on in a dense, treacly flow across the roadways and the traffic-islands, past immobilized cars and buses, until it came to the cordon. The police, with linked arms, strove to hold it back, but still it flowed. The line of police, scrabbling for foothold, bent in a bow, and finally broke. A scattered cheer arose from further back, and the crowd flowed on down Whitehall with its banners and placards tossing on the flood.

Presently the front ranks began to sing. Further back, too, the song was taken up:

Diana Brackley's body lies a-murdered in her grave,
Diana Brackley's body lies a-murdered in her grave,
Diana Brackley's body lies a-murdered in her grave,
Her work goes marching on!

As the crowd drained out of the Square more people flooded in from the streets to follow on behind. Passengers on stranded buses got out to join, too.

The volume of the singing increased as the head of the procession passed the end of Downing Street:

Shoot us if you want to as they shot Diana down,
Her work will still go on!

There was another cordon at the far end of Whitehall, stronger than the first, but it, too, sagged before the pressure, and gave way. The crowd flowed out, over Parliament Square.

From somewhere a loudspeaker roared ponderously:

"WE—WANT—THE—ANTI-GEE!"

giving the rhythm. The crowd took it up, and its multivoiced chant rebounded in echoes from the Abbey to the Government Offices, from the Central Hall to the face of the Houses of Parliament:

"WE—WANT—THE—ANTI-GEE!"
"WE—WANT—THE—ANTI-GEE!"

—

"The P.M. was impressed. He admitted it," Lydia Washington told Janet Tewley. "'A performance quite in the historic tradition of demonstrations,' he called it.

"So I said to him: 'Well, there it is, Willy. What are you going to do? Are you going to take notice? Or are you going to send me away to turn the League for the New Life into a political party which will fight you tooth and nail at the next election? Or, of course, there is the third possibility of civil commotion: what our grandmothers could do, we can do.'

"'My dear Lydia,' he said, 'I am against civil commotion. It is costly and untidy, and I am even more opposed to it since resistance movements have given people ideas that your grandmother never thought of. Also, I confess, our side of the House would regret to see a new, and, possibly, very popular Party arise. The Opposition, I am sure, would regret it still more: they are deeply riven by this business already, you know. It is not impossible that some of their quite prominent figures might come over to you: there is a dated—dare I say, arrested?—quality in their far left that many of their intellectuals find extremely trying at the best of times. So I think we may say that they would rather lose to us than be split by a new challenger.

"'Our own Party is, one must admit, far from single-minded in this matter. Many seem not to have learned, even yet, that if you turn your face away from Science, she will land you a mule's kick on your backside. Nevertheless, in view of the alternatives, I have no doubt that we could put it through—*if* it lay within our power to do so.'"

Janet frowned.

"What did he mean by that?"

"He had received a letter—he showed it to me—written from some hospital by a Dr. Saxover who, he assured me, is a well-known biologist—or was it biochemist?—something of that kind, anyway. The letter was dated last Monday, two days after Diana's death. This Dr. Saxover said that he knew all about the Antigerone, and had been making it for years, though not for Diana, but he had been holding it back in the hope of finding some alternative source-material. It came, he said, from a lichen growing only, as far as he knew, in North Manchuria—the P.M. told me his own reports confirmed that—but he went on to say that he had that morning received an air letter from his agent in Hong Kong telling him that the Chinese authorities had initiated a large new collective farm in a district which included the whole of the known lichen-bearing area, and that the plowing up was already in hand. To the best of Dr. Saxover's belief there had never been more of the lichen than would supply the quantity of the Lichenin Antigerone that would be needed by three or four thousand people. Now there would be none! Consequently, no more of the Antigerone could be produced.

"'An artless man, this Dr. Saxover,' said the P.M. 'He appears to regard the development as a coincidence.'

"'Which you do not?' I said.

"'So far,' he remarked, 'the rest of the world has not taken this very seriously—rather as if it were a silly-season stunt, with just, perhaps, the merest atom of something somewhere in it. But the

Chinese are a very subtle people. Also they have an excellent Intelligence Service. Observe how convenient this is for them. Quite fortuitously all the lichen, which could have caused a great deal of trouble, has disappeared. No need to say anything but velly solly. It won't do anyone any good to raise a rumpus about stuff that no longer exists, will it! Furthermore, their own over-population problem is already serious; if they were to add longevity to their remarkable fecundity the country would very soon burst at all seams.

" 'One may doubt,' he added, thoughtfully, 'whether quite *all* the lichen will have gone under. It will be interesting to notice whether any of their leaders shows signs of wearing unusually well during the coming years. However, be that as it may, the lichen is certainly put out of anyone else's reach. And that leaves us with *our* problems.'

" 'It certainly does, Willy,' I agreed. 'In fact it is just about as conveniently pat for your government, isn't it? So convenient that nobody is going to believe it—which is not going to do you, or your Party, or any of us, any good."

"He agreed, but he said:

" 'Well, what do you suggest? We can't *grow* the stuff for them. Even if this fellow Saxover could let Kew have spores from it— it is spores that lichen uses?—anyhow, if Kew could develop it, it would take many years to start such a scheme, and even then it is doubtful whether it could be produced in anything like sufficient quantity.'

" 'Nevertheless,' I told him, 'something must be done, Willy. In this case, at any rate, it certainly isn't true that what you've never had, you never miss. Now that we've got them all worked up, they'll miss it all right; want to fight the Chinese, most likely. They'll bawl like a child who's had its toy snatched away— What's the matter . . . ?' I said, for he'd suddenly opened his eyes wide.

" 'You've got it, Lydia,' he told me, beaming.

" 'I only said—'

" 'What *do* you say to pacify a child who's lost a favorite toy?'

" 'Why—"don't cry, darling. I'll buy you another." '

" 'Exactly,' he told me, and beamed again."

—

"As listeners to our later bulletins will have already heard, the Prime Minister addressed the House last night on the subject of the Antigerone.

"The Government had, he said, for some little time been giving this matter their gravest consideration. If their announcement should have seemed to the public to be somewhat delayed, that must be put down to an earnest desire to raise no false hopes. The stage had now been reached, however, when it was desirable that the people should be acquainted with the facts. They were these. The discovery of the Antigerone was a scientific triumph which was again showing the world that British research was second to none. Unfortunately, however, it did not follow that when you had made a discovery you had found an infinite quantity of your discovery. On the contrary, many substances could only be produced at first with great difficulty, and at great cost. He would instance aluminum which was on its first appearance rarer than, and, as a result, more costly than, platinum. The present state of the Antigerone was not dissimilar from that. At present it would only be derived in minute quantities from an extremely rare form of lichen. The Government had consulted eminent scientists in attempts to discover methods by which the output could be raised to a degree where it was readily available for all. Unfortunately, again, the scientists could hold out no immediate prospects of improvement. It was, however, the Government's firm intention that this state of affairs should be remedied as soon as possible.

"The Government, therefore, proposed an immediate grant of ten million pounds to subsidize research to this end.

"He had little doubt, indeed our record of scientific progress assured him that he need have *no* doubt, that British brains, British purpose, and British know-how would succeed—and succeed in the very near future—in producing a supply of the Antigerone for every man and woman in the country who wishes to use it. . . ."

15

Francis Saxover stopped his car at the point where a whitegated lane led off from the secondary road. On the top bar of the gate was neatly lettered: GLEN FARM. By turning a little more left, he could see the house. A comfortable-looking house that belonged in the scene, built of gray local stone, perhaps three centuries ago, seeming almost to grow out of the hillside. It rested on a small shelf, looking out across the lake from shining, white-framed windows, a small garden, now in the chrysanthemum stage, immediately before it, the fell rising steeply behind. On its north side some lower outbuildings linked it to a large barn. Blue smoke rose from one of the two chimney stacks, and drifted back toward the fellside. A farm, undoubtedly; equally without doubt, not a working farm.

After some moments' contemplation of it he got out, opened the gate, and took his car through. He drove up slowly, parked where the lane widened, close to the house, and sat there for a moment before he got out.

He did not approach the house at once, but walked thoughtfully to the edge of the leveled shelf, where he stood looking across the garden and the placid sheet of water beyond. He remained there in unmoving contemplation for almost a minute. Then, as he made to turn, something close to his feet caught his attention. He regarded it for some seconds, and then bent to pick it up. He looked at it expressionlessly, as it lay in the palm of his hand. Then the corner of his mouth twitched slightly. He let the piece of lichen drop, and turned toward the house.

A staunch-looking country girl opened the door.

"Mrs. Ingles?" Francis inquired.

"I think she's in the barn, sir. I'll tell her. What would be the name?"

"Oh, just say I'm from the County Rating Authority," he told her.

He was shown into a large, low, comfortable sitting-room: white paint, gray walls, a few excellent flower pictures, wood embers smoldering beneath a polished copper canopy in the fireplace. He was looking out of the window when the door opened.

"Good morning—" the familiar voice began.

Francis turned.

"Oh—!" she exclaimed. Then more faintly, "Oh—!" And she swayed . . .

"That was a silly thing to do," Diana said unsteadily, as she came round. "Oh, God, I'm going to cry." She did. "I'm not a cryer, I'm not," she said through it. "Nobody ever makes me cry but you. Oh, hell!"

Ten minutes later, and somewhat restored, she said:

"But how did you know, Francis? . . . And how did you know where to look?"

"My dear, I was not, as they say, born yesterday. There was nothing wrong with the act. It was a superb piece of sharp practice. But there were indications—your sudden visit to Darr, for instance, your manner, certain choices of phrase. Finding out about Mrs. Ingles who lived here was more difficult, and complicated to begin with by my misapprehension that I was looking for an unnamed lady who had recently gone abroad."

"I've taken some trouble over getting Mrs. Ingles well established here," said Diana. "It was less difficult than it might have been, though, because I am Mrs. Ingles."

Francis stared at her, taken aback.

"That certainly did not occur to me. In fact, I understood you to tell me you were not married. Is he—are you—?"

Diana shook her head.

"When I say I *am* Mrs. Ingles, I mean I *could* be by common parlance—though I must say the practice of divorcing one's husband but hanging on to his surname strikes me as pretty moot." She paused, then went on: "It was a long time ago. When you are young, when you have been shocked, when what you really wanted has gone beyond your reach, you're apt to look rather desperately for a new way of living. That doesn't make a good basis for marriage. It was brief—and unhappy while it lasted . . . So I didn't try marriage again . . . I had set myself a job—and, mostly, I stuck to it . . . It's kept me pretty busy. . . ."

"And are you satisfied with the job, now?" Francis asked.

She turned her gray eyes steadily on him.

"I know you disapprove. 'Sharp practice' you said just now—and I'm aware that that is a mild, polite term compared with what a lot of people would be saying, if they knew . . .

"All right: it *was* an unscrupulous piece of manipulation. I don't care what names it is called. There are things that are too important, too *necessary,* for a few conventional scruples to stand in their way; and, for me, this is one of them. I'm not proud of the means, but I'm satisfied with the job—so far. There *could* have been bloodshed—even something like civil war—but we've got this far without any of that.

"When people have had time to think it over there'll be more trouble, lots of it probably; but it's too late for that to matter much—the children have been promised their sweets, and they'll raise hell if they're not forthcoming. But they will forthcome. Both the Americans and the Russians have now made bigger allocations for research than we have; they must have hated doing it, but, there you are; we started it, and a nation's science simply has to keep up with the Joneses these days.

"The *real* trouble will come later on. We *may* get through that without bloodshed too, but it won't be easy. If we wake up to the famine problem *now,* if we work flat out on ways to increase food supplies, if something can be done to discourage the suicidal birthrate, we might just manage it with no more trouble than discomforts and short rations for a time. We shall see. All I care about is that we've got *homo diuturnus,* or *homo vivax,* or whatever they'll call him, on stage, and waiting in the wings."

She paused. She regarded Francis's face carefully for nearly half a minute, and then turned her own away.

"*You're* shocked! *You!*" she exclaimed. "I wonder how your shock compares with the shock to a young woman who finds that, or thinks she finds that—oh, I'm still not really clear which—finds that the—the central ethic of her calling is being— being violated by—by . . . Oh, God, are you going to *make* me say it, Francis . . . ?"

—

When the sun, setting behind the opposite mountains, brought shadows creeping across the lake, Francis's car was still parked beside Glen Farm. Within the house, the really important decisions had been taken, but, on the couch before the fire, lesser points of merely general importance continued to raise themselves.

"This ten millions," Diana said pensively. "I don't trust politicians."

"All right, I think," Francis told her. "For one thing, there are some good individual awards to be won. But, more importantly,

Lydia Washington has got Janet Tewley as well as herself onto the Committee. I don't see either of those two letting any fiddling get by."

"In the meantime, though, have you any reserves of lichenin?"

"Enough to keep Zephanie, Paul, Richard, and myself going for some time. I gave you the rest for research purposes. And you?"

"Quite a bit. It's got to do for Sarah and Lucy, and several others. Also, there are Janet, and Lydia, and some more that I shall have to do something about unless the researches produce results within two or three years. I can't let them down altogether."

"Which would mean letting them know you're still alive."

"They'd be almost bound to find out, sooner or later."

"When were you going to let me know?"

"Oh, Francis, don't! That was the worst part. I don't think I could have held out very long."

"And if there are no results in, say, three years, you will have a new supply?" he asked.

"Oh, you noticed that, did you? Yes, it seems to have taken here quite well, but, of course, it won't be possible to produce more than a very little—the same old problem."

They sat looking at the flames licking the logs. Francis said:

"All the way through this I heard no expectation mentioned but two hundred years—no suggestion of anything else. Why did you stick to that?"

"Why did you use a factor of three for Zephanie and Paul?"

"Mostly because a bigger factor would certainly have aroused their suspicions sooner. It could have been increased later, if I'd managed the synthesis, and been able to publish."

"For much the same reason I kept the factor down with the clients. Then when it came to publicizing it—well, two hundred seemed a nice, comprehensible sort of number. Enough improvement to make them want it, but not so much that it would intimidate them."

"Does it intimidate you, Diana?"

"It used to, sometimes. But now not. Nothing could intimidate me now, Francis—except the prospect of not having long enough..."

Francis reached for her hand.

"This isn't going to be very easy, you know," he told her. "You certainly can't simply reappear again after all this. Heaven knows what would happen to you. So, even if I were to decide to rebuild Darr, we couldn't go there. I suppose it means that we shall have to go abroad somewhere...."

"Oh, I've got all *that* arranged," said Diana. "We can stay here. It's a nice house, don't you think? You'll have married Mrs. Ingles. You did it quietly because if it were known that Mrs. Ingles was Diana Brackley's younger sister, there would naturally be a lot of publicity, which neither of you wanted. For the same reason, you both decided to go on living here quietly for a few years. There's lots of room, Francis; I'll show you round after dinner. I've often thought the room over the dining-room would make a lovely nursery. Well, then when you become a public figure again, we've only got to stick quite firmly to the poor-Diana's-younger-sister line. People will get used to it, and—"

"Incidentally. Poor Diana was shot three times. What of her wounds?"

"Blanks, darling—And a little thing they sometimes use on television. You wear it under your clothes, and when you press it, red ink spurts out, frightfully gruesome-looking. Well, as I was saying—"

"What you were saying, Diana, was something about my becoming 'a public figure again.' Now, in the first place I never was, as far as I know, a public figure at all—"

"Well, you're terribly well-known, Francis. I should have

thought—oh, we won't argue about that. The point is that we can't both sit down here and do nothing for two or three hundred years, can we? That's what everyone's going to find out. In fact, it's the whole object of the exercise.

"I've got quite a nice lab fixed up in the barn, so we can work there. That's where *you* are going to determine the basic molecule of the antigerone—which will certainly make you a public figure . . . Come along, darling. I'll show you . . ."

ABOUT THE AUTHOR

JOHN WYNDHAM PARKES LUCAS BEYNON HARRIS was born in Knowle, Warwickshire, England, on July 10, 1903. The recent discovery of his personal papers has shed light on the previously unknown life of Wyndham. Until 1911, he lived in Edgbaston, Birmingham, England, and then moved to other parts of the country. After attending several private preparatory schools, he enrolled in Bedales School in Petersfield, England, about an hour's drive from London. He began writing short stories in 1925 after unsuccessful attempts at careers in farming, law, advertising, and commercial art, and through the 1930s made his living by selling his stories to a myriad of periodicals. When England entered World War II, Wyndham joined the English civil service and later the British Army. After leaving the army in 1946, he resumed his writing, turning to novels and publishing under many different pseudonyms. The 1950s brought him great financial and critical success with *The Day of the Triffids* (1951), *The Kraken Wakes* (1953), *The Chrysalids* (1955), and *The Midwich Cuckoos* (1957). He died on March 11, 1969.

ABOUT THE TYPE

The principal text of this Modern Library edition was set in a digitized version of Janson, a typeface that dates from about 1690 and was cut by Nicholas Kis (1650–1702), a Hungarian working in Amsterdam. The original matrices have survived and are held by the Stempel foundry in Germany. Hermann Zapf (1918–2015) redesigned some of the weights and sizes for Stempel, basing his revisions on the original design.